GARY PHILLIPS'

HOLLIS
FOR HIRE

GARY PHILLIPS - PHILLIP DRAYER DUNCAN - SARAH M. CHEN
SARA PARETSKY - SCOTT ADLERBERG - NAOMI HIRAHARA

PRO SE ⚖ PRESS™

PRO SE ⚖ PRESS

GARY PHILLIPS' HOLLIS FOR HIRE
A Pro Se Productions Publication

Hollywood Killer by Gary Phillips
A King's Game by Phillip Drayer Duncan
King Cow by Gary Phillips
A Trip to School by Scott Adlerberg
The Parachute Kids by Sarah M. Chen
The Case of the Missing Dentist by Gary Phillips
Reparations by Naomi Hirahara
White Out by Sara Paretsky

Editing by Gary Phillips, Kristi King-Morgan, Katiana Uyemura
Cover by Jeffrey Hayes
Book Design by Antonino Lo Iacono & Marzia Marina
New Pulp Logo Design by Sean E. Ali
New Pulp Seal Design by Cari Reese

www.prose-press.com

GARY PHILLIPS' HOLLIS FOR HIRE

CONTENTS

HOLLYWOOD KILLER

by
Gary Phillips

The Dread Knight ran along the alleyway, rivulets of sweat seeping from beneath his mask. He plowed into a knot of plastic garbage bags and soggy cardboard boxes propped against the wall. The trash went flying and the costumed man nearly lost his balance. Seeking to regain his footing, his boots got tangled up in his flowing gray mesh cape and he tore at it to remove the damn thing. But he'd done too good a job of double-stitching the heavy duty material to the cowling, and he couldn't remove his cape.

"Oh, shit," the Dread Knight swore, looking back, panic distorting his blue eyes through his eye slits. Maybe he'dp lost his pursuer. He started running again and almost got to the end of the alley when he felt a tug on his cape from behind. Like a slapstick bit in a Farley Bothers movie, his feet went out from under him and he landed hard on his backside.

"No, come on, please," the Dread Knight said, holding out a hand in a defensive gesture. "Help me!" he screamed. "Somebody help me."

The first shot punched through the side of his neck and his mouth gaped in pain. The second shot ended his agony as the bullet burrowed itself just off-center in his forehead.

***

Nate Hollis sat against the headboard reading the paperback version of *House of Cards* by William Cohan, about the collapse of Bear Sterns. He was clad in plaid pajama pants. Next to him, wearing the top that matched his pants, was Kristy Simons. Several years older than her private investigator paramour, Simons was the publisher of a political and cultural blog, along with its hardcopy weekly tabloid version, the *L.A. Voice*. She was texting on her BlackBerry.

"Darling," she murmured, sending a reply to her reporter Ronnie Harper who'd sent her a message. "I have bad news for you."

Hollis looked at her expectantly. "What's that, baby?"

"Your superhero, the one you have all those silly reprint tradepapers of?" She gripped his shoulder. "The Dread Knight is dead. Killed in a funky alley off Fountain. His arch-enemy, the Reigning Fool, is the key suspect."

He screwed up his face at her.

"I suppose it's bad taste to go on," she said. "That was from Ronnie. He's on scene at the apparent murder of one of those wannabes who dress up as costumed characters and panhandle tourists on the Boulevard."

"Huh. Robbery?"

"It seems. Ronnie says the cops found his wallet a block away, empty of cash, but his driver's license was in it. I guess he didn't have it secured in his utility belt." She said this straight-faced. "The Knight's real name was Donald Frees. Mr. Harper is digging up more."

Hollis shook his head and put his book aside. "So it has come to this, the never-ending, never satisfied salacious hunger of the gossip starved hoi polloi has to be fed with who ain't wearing underwear, what drug cocktail has done in the pop star, and who done did in one of these pathetic dress up mufus."

She placed a purple-nailed hand on his bare chest, tenderly kneading the area. Simons put aside her BlackBerry as well. "Funny, I'm not wearing underwear either."

"Do tell." They grinned lasciviously at each other and made love again.

***

Two days later, Patrolman Second Grade Barry Yargroff stepped through a homeless encampment under the Hollywood

Freeway overpass on Argyle. He hated this detail. He knew times were tough, but the businesses in the area had been complaining to the Watch Commander and so here he was with wary, bleary eyes on him.

He tapped his T-handled nightstick against the edge of a plastic milk crate. "Okay, good people, you need to get up and get going." Groans and farts sounded. "I know this is messed up, but that's the deal and there's no debate."

"Where the hell are we supposed to go, man? Church is full." The woman who spoke was squat, heavyset with frizzed out dishwater blonde hair and wearing a bandolier containing cooking utensils. The church she referred to was a nearby Methodist denomination run by an activist pastor that also had a small shelter.

Yargroff spread his arms wide. "What can I tell you, beautiful? I'm not the housing authority. But none of you are virgins to the streets, you'll manage. But it just can't be here. Let's hop to it, por favor." More grumbling and a shifting of the rank odor hanging about the area like a heavy fog. A few began placing their meager belongings in various types of carts or wagons. The woman with the bandolier stood and pulled on the stuffed and stained duffle bag she'd been sitting cross-legged on. Three days from now Patrolman Yargroff knew they'd be back, but that would be his day off and some other on-duty's problem.

He walked about, making lifting motions with his hands to keep them from getting distracted. Particularly those who should be in a mental care facility. But where was the money for that in a city and county reeling from one budget crisis to the next?

"Rapido, rapido," Yargroff said. A rat skittered into view and reared back on its hind legs, twitching its nose at him. The rodent stood in front of a pair of feet belonging to someone stretched out on a dark blanket. The feet were clad in stylish red boots with high heels. Yargroff came closer, the rat skittering away. It was a woman lying face down in an outfit of black mesh stockings and tight black shortie shorts. And was that a cape tied around her neck? *A crack ho with a gimmick*, Yargroff assessed while he tapped his nightstick against the soles of her feet. Though he did note this woman looked to be in shape, none of that fried chicken at two a.m. fat hanging over her waistline.

"Ma'am, I need you to raise up from your slumber. I've got to

3

GARY PHILLIPS

clear this place out." No movement, no snoring, nothing. He bent and shook her shoulder. Cold. Too cold, especially on a hot day like today. He felt for the pulse in her neck. "Don't anybody move," he hollered, his hand going for his Rover to call in his discovery.

"Make up your mind," a man with no front teeth whistled. "Go. Stay. Which is it?"

"Quiet," the officer commanded. "This is zero-six-dub-u-thirty-five with a DB," he said into his radio, also giving his location and requesting a plainclothes from his sergeant, who would send a black and white as well. He severed the call. The dead woman's face was turned such he could see part of it in profile. The deceased, Asian, was in her mid-twenties he estimated, heavy green eye shadow beneath a domino mask. She had long straight raven black hair. He rose and began walking to the perimeter to make sure no one lumbered off. He removed some three by five index cards from his flapped shirt pocket to begin taking statements.

"It is she, the one," a rail thin man in a '70s disco get-up with a bald head and round tinted eyeglasses said, staring at the body.

Yargroff frowned at him. This civilian was 60 at least, he guessed. "You know this woman?"

The bald man outstretched his arms like an evangelist cajoling his congregation. "She is the one, true goddess of pain and justice delivered by the Viking Queen. She is the deliverer of the ebon fires of righteousness and redemption. She is the Black Flame." He went to his knees and supplicated before her, his hands shaking rhythmically.

Smiling satisfactorily, Yargroff handcuffed his suspect.

***

"Kobe ain't got nothin' on Jerry West," Obadiah Hollis said to his grandson. "That boy's too damn moody."

Nate Hollis swallowed some of his pastrami sandwich, sitting across from the owner of the Hideaway bar and grill. He jabbed his pickle slice at his forbearer. "Jerry only has one ring. You do know how many Kobe has?"

"Shuh," the old man huffed. "Rings don't tell the whole story."

4

Their bantering continued as two pretty twentysomething women entered the tavern in the Crenshaw District. One was white, the other African American. They came over to the two men.

"Ladies," the older man said, bowing slightly from where he stood behind the bar. "Yes, that's right, I am the famous Clutch Hollis."

Nate Hollis snickered. "Don't mind him. Too many hits to the head when he played." Framed photostats behind the bar from various sports pages attested to the pro football career of Obadiah "Clutch" Hollis who played linebacker for the Rams in the sixties. There were other pictures of him with celebrities such as Red Foxx and Eartha Kitt. There was also several shots of his dead son, Earl, Nate's father, a plainclothesman murdered, the mystery so far unsolved.

"I'm Eva Payton," the black woman said, shaking both Hollis' hands. "And this is Linda Brenner," she added, indicating her friend who also shook hands.

"We need you to find out who murdered our friend, Mr. Hollis." Brenner declared, her mouth set hard.

"We googled L.A. private eyes and read about some of your cases. You used to be an investigator for the DA. We chose you hoping you might have a line into the police."

Clutch Hollis chuckled. "Oh, yeah, Sam Pope is a big fan of his. That's why Mister District Attorney had him bounced."

"Let's sit over here." Nate Hollis got off the stool and led the way to a back table in the bar. At this time in the afternoon, there were only a few patrons in having a late lunch.

Sitting across from each other, Payton produced a laptop from the messenger bag slung around her shoulders and placed it open on the round table. "The three of us are...were, roommates," she began, powering up her computer.

"The old story of coming out to Hollywood to make it," Brenner contributed. "Me and Eva are behind the camera, but Willow," she stopped herself, choking up.

"That's okay, take your time," Hollis said.

"The police have arrested a homeless man, a former mental patient, we understand," Payton said.

"Based on what?" Hollis asked.

5

"His behavior, as far as we could tell from what the police detective who came to see us said." She told him about the strange way the suspect acted under the freeway overpass where their friend's body was found.

Brenner crossed her arms defensively as if warding off bad omens. "Willow was stabbed in her stomach but they haven't found the knife or anything like that on this guy they arrested."

"When was the last time you two had seen her?"

"The day before she was found," Brenner answered. "Willow worked at the Book Soup bookstore on Sunset. She had a signing there that night she was responsible for.'

Hollis asked, "Didn't you think it was odd she didn't come home after that?"

The two women looked at each other sheepishly.

"I spent the night over my boyfriend's place," Brenner said.

"And I was pulling an all-nighter in the editing bay on a commercial I'd snagged at the last minute," Payton added. "The facility's in the Valley so I crashed there for a couple of hours to get the job done on time."

Payton continued, "But we have a theory on who killed her given she was found in her costume."

"Costume?"

Payton turned the laptop around for Hollis to see the monitor. On it was a video of a tall Asian woman with the unforced air of a model. She laughed and flitted about for the camera in the kind of skimpy outfit teenage boys and middle-aged men salivate over. He frowned, recalling the violent death of Frees from several days ago. "Your friend Willow."

"Willow Ahn," Payton said. "As you can see, she was gorgeous and funny. She'd had a couple of small parts in some C level horror movies and we decided to do a kind of reality show-like project with her to get her, well, all of us, some attention." The clip changed to show Willow Ahn in costume talking to some others in superhero attire, from a man in an insect costume with curved antennae on his head, to a muscular large woman in a modified ancient gladiator costume. The group sat at two tables pushed together in a noisy restaurant. The volume was low but Hollis could hear the ersatz icons grousing about their bad tips, long hours, and little kids socking them in the crotch to see how tough they were.

Payton said, "We came up with the idea of her being one of those would-be entertainers on Hollywood Boulevard staking out the theaters pretending to be these comics characters."

"A way to have her play this part yet also give us a look at the underside of tinsel town," Brenner put in. "She chose the Black Flame as the character was Chinese American in the comics." She hunched her shoulders. "Well, there were no Korean characters she liked."

Hollis pointed at Payton. "You're the director?"

"Yes, and Linda is the producer-writer."

Payton's camera had settled on a white male whose facial features were a close approximation of illustrated versions Hollis remembered from his teen years of comics collecting. The subject was staring at Ahn, who was talking off camera. "Who's the one playing Doc Jupiter, Hero of the Space Age?"

"Michael, goes by Mickey, Stratham," Brenner remarked harshly. "You can see it in his eyes, can't you? The expression on his face."

Hollis held up a hand. "Him giving your friend the wolf leer doesn't make him her killer. I mean, you said it, she was fine."

Payton froze the image. "He's a real creep. Stratham's had cut work done to his face to look like Doc Jupiter, pec implants and, ah…"

"Penile enlargement," her friend finished, disgusted. "And he's a gun nut." Her final indictment.

"Well, Willow was stabbed. But check this out." Payton cued up another segment of her unfinished documentary. On screen was a pan of a room crammed with all kinds of Doc Jupiter memorabilia, from bobble heads, statuettes, and a scale model of the Hero of the Space Age's mountain top headquarters, to water gun rifles with the Doc Jupiter logo, beach towels and so on.

"Not only is he obsessed with being Doc Jupiter," Brenner said, "but the asshole claims to be the illegitimate son of Roger Kyles."

Hollis looked at her blankly.

"Kyles played the character in a syndicated TV show in the eighties."

"Has this has been disproven?"

"Kyles died in a boating accident but was known to have fathered a couple of kids by Jupiter groupies. So conveniently he's not around to protest, and his offspring do their best to ignore Stratham."

"How does Stratham's weirdness tie to your friend?"

Payton fast-forwarded then came to a scene where Stratham was tapping his finger on the cover of a comic book encased in plastic. On it was a rendering of the wedding of Doc Jupiter and the Black Flame.

"A damn crossover event between Imperium and MK Comics twenty years ago," Brenner noted as Payton turned up the volume.

"See, Willow, we were intended for each other," Stratham was saying. "It was predicted, and I can make it come true." Payton zoomed in on Stratham's lopsided smile, showing his far too even capped teeth.

***

Forty-three-year-old Donald Frees, aka the Dread Knight, wasn't in the restaurant scene Payton had shot. She did have a clip of him in civilian clothes at his other job, the shift manager of a Chicken Delight fried chicken stand in Koreatown. He knew Willow Ahn in passing, but there seemed to be no deeper connection to them or their deaths other than both being in the costume trade. Her for the exposure and him, in his own words, because just maybe he could inspire one kid to be an upstanding citizen. Then, there was the two different methods of death. That didn't necessarily mean two different killers, Hollis reflected, driving along Hollywood Boulevard. He'd encountered enough malefactors who liked to vary their mayhem.

"Thanks, Ronnie," he said, thumbing off his cell after talking with the *Voice*'s reporter. Harper had interviewed Frees' widow. The reporter learned that her husband and Stratham had had a run in over a bit part – essentially playing themselves playing the comics characters. This for a low budget straight-to-video effort. According to her, Stratham had tried to poison the well by having friends call the producer, alleging Frees had a drug problem and was unreliable.

"Hey now, all right then." The Hero of the Space Age grinned and flexed, as the father in cargo shorts took the picture of him with his arm around his son. He whispered to the father, "I can't charge a fee, but if you want to tip me…"

The father sucked his front teeth and handed over a five. Doc Jupiter tucked it away behind his wide belt and stared off, searching for another customer. Hollis had watched this in front of the Galaxy Theater complex. He had to veer around an individual stomping about in an Itor, the Indestructible rubber suit, to intercept Stratham.

"Need a moment, Mr. Stratham."

The man, dressed in jodhpurs and a double-breasted tunic with epaulets, regarded Hollis' snap brim hat, small hoop earring and his timeless casual attire. "You dress too good to be a cop."

"I want to talk to you about the murder of Willow Ahn."

He sneered. "PI, huh? Them stuck up bitches hired you."

"I just have a few questions. Like where were you the night of the 18th?" That was the night of Ahn's signing.

The muscular Stratham grabbed Hollis' elbow, tugging him away from the people milling about. "What the fuck's wrong with you? There's already rumors going around about some nut out to eliminate his costumed completion, and you show up at my place of work with this bullshit."

Hollis pulled his arm away. "I'm told you were obsessive about Willow Ahn. Texting her with inappropriate jokes, making sure you got in a lot of her shots."

"You didn't look like no choirboy, dog. You gay, that it?" He bared those even teeth. "You never tried to get with a woman?"

"You fall by the bookstore after closing, Mickey? Maybe you convinced Willow to have a drink with you, told her how bad you felt about pushing up on her. Drugged her, helped her outside like she was drunk, then took her to your place so you could dress her up and play out your sick fantasies?"

Stratham shoved Hollis. "Fuck you. Get out of here."

Hollis touched the brim of his hat. "Guess I'll try out my idea with my cop buddies. I checked your record, home, you've been arrested for assault before." He turned and Stratham roared, coming at him.

"You better stay the hell out of my business," he yelled. He swung at Hollis who ducked, the man's fist connecting on the back of the detective's ear. Hollis staggered, his hat falling off. Stratham pressed his attack as the crowd gawked.

Hollis got his arms around the other man's waist and the two grunted and grappled, each trying to get a decisive blow on the other but mostly pummeling each other's back and sides. Hollis brought his head up, clipping the fake adventurer under the jaw. This relaxed his hold on him and Hollis straightened up and drove a fist into Stratham's stomach, who countered with a blow to Hollis' jaw.

The hit dazed the investigator but he fought through the haze descending on his brain and tagged Stratham with a straight right that made the other man's eye go glassy for a moment. Hollis took advantage. A short jab back under that tender chin sent Stratham stumbling into some onlookers who helped him up.

"Mommy, mommy," a little girl pointed. "The bad man hurt the Mister Jupiter." Her little brother next her started crying.

"Aw, jeez," Hollis groused.

The children's mother tried to comfort her distraught children as she glared at him. Breathing heavily, he picked up his hat, eyes on his opponent. Stratham was also breathing hard. He didn't make a move.

***

Plainclothes LAPD Detective Maynard Regus' second rapid knock sounded on the door. It was to the top floor abode of a Spanish-Mediterranean-style duplex in the Fairfax District. "Come on, champ," the baritone voiced man growled. "Let's not wake up everybody, shall we?"

A sleepy Nate Hollis opened the door on the cop accompanied by two uniforms. He was in sweats and an athletic tee. He rubbed his close shaven head. "The fuck, man?" It was three-forty in the morning.

"You gonna let me in, playboy?"

Hollis left the door ajar and sat on the arm of his couch. On the coffee table was a small pile of several days of the *Los Angeles Times*, last week's *L.A. Voice*, and the Cohan book.

The uniformed officers took positions in the background, one of them before the framed and signed large print by photographer

Neil Leifer of a gloating Muhammad Ali standing over a downed Sonny Liston.

The mustachioed Regus stood over Hollis, hands in his pockets. Dramatically he looked toward the bedroom, twitching his eyebrows, and whispered, "We alone?"

"Yes," Hollis drawled.

"Guess why I'm here."

Hollis stretched and yawned.

"Michael Stratham was ambushed earlier tonight. Shot coming home from an appearance at one of those collector's shows over in Burbank." Regus beamed. "He's in a bad way over at Kaiser."

"I forget 'cause I got so many gats. What I shoot him with?" He folded his arms.

"Looks like a .38 slug."

"Same as what killed Donald Frees."

The humor left Regus' face.

Hollis put his hands on his knees. "What? You really didn't think you had me, did you? That I was seeking revenge after me and Stratham's tete-a-tete this afternoon?" He sat back, folding his arms. "So, he fingered me from his hospital bed?"

Regus worried his lips, his thick mustache going crooked. "He's under sedation, not talking yet. Tracing his prior movements, there was a report from one of our bike patrols about a fight on the Boulevard. One of the participants, male, black, mid-thirties, driving away in a cherry ragtop dark green '60s era car." Hollis drove a 1969 Dodge Dart. Regus leaned in. "Where'd you go after your sparring session?"

"To the bookstore where Willow Ahn worked to see if Stratham or anybody else came to see her." Absently, Hollis rubbed his split knuckle.

"And?"

"He didn't. Ahn did go out for drinks with several people who'd come to see Clemments at the book signing."

"Who?"

"Alister Clemments."

"Who?"

Hollis sighed. "The horror actor. You know, *The Thousand Guillotines of Dr. Vulcanus, Nazi Pirates of the Haunted Reef,* played vampires, mad scientists, etcetera, etcetera."

"So maybe he's going around doing these killings, huh?"

"He's eighty if he's a day."

"He can probably turn into a bat or smoke and fly around the city swooping down on young, firm babes." Regus seemed pleased with that image in his head.

"So where do you think Willow Ahn was killed before her body was dumped?"

Regus removed his hands from his pockets as he paced about. "What gave you that idea?"

"Alister Clemments didn't kill that girl. He's got the palsy and can't weigh a hundred and ten holding two buckets of water – if he could hold the two buckets. She was knifed before she was dressed in her costume. But no signs of sexual molestation. Then whoever did it had to lift her and put her in a car. Willow wasn't petite and Clemments has no car or seemingly access to one."

Regus gazed at a reproduction of a Lucian Freud self-portrait on the wall. "Still got a few friends in the coroner's office. I like that about you, Hollis." He signaled with a jerk of his head to the uniforms it was time to go. "You're a pain in the ass to everybody."

Hollis made a gesture as the four moved to the door. "Hey, what about I give you some information, you throw me a bone. Like your theory on what ties these three attacks together."

"Keep your nose clean, peeper." The policemen departed.

Hollis went into the kitchen and drank some orange juice from the bottle. He then tried to go back to sleep, but it wouldn't take. Over and over he wondered about the use of the same gun on Frees and Stratham, but then the change up and the knife used on Willow Ahn. Allowing for the supposition it was the same person in the three incidents, what did the switch mean?

The kind of gun used in the crimes was interesting too. It was an old school piece, the caliber of the bullet suggesting a revolver or a Walther P-38, an automatic used by the Germans in World War II. There was also an American version of a .38 auto by Colt. Following up on what Brenner has said, he'd confirmed that Stratham was a gun collector. So, some connection there? But the knife was personal. The pistol was business, but the use of that blade could be someone who could get close to Willow Ahn— close to surprise her.

After an hour of no slumber, Hollis got out of bed, returned to the kitchen, and put on some coffee. Waiting for the stuff to brew, he played parts of the now aborted Black Flame reality show his clients had been putting together. Payton had given him a copy. Sipping his coffee, he paused the DVD on his laptop several times at the restaurant scene. Utilizing screen capture, he produced printout shots of the people around the table.

Looking at his pictures and despite the coffee, Hollis felt tired and was able to get a few hours of sleep before he was up again at eight with a plan for the day. He made several calls, including talking to one of his clients and revisiting the bookstore. But the assistant manager he'd talked to the other day was off. The employees wouldn't give her phone number, but did pass his email along to her and she contacted him. He scanned pdf's of his screen captures on his combo fax/printer and sent those to the assistant manager. He drove over to a bar called the Winter Palace in West Hollywood, then took a trip the Chicken Delight Frees managed on 6th Street in Koreatown. The kid at the counter called another youngster over, no more than twenty-three or so. His name was Mike Yuan, and he'd been promoted to temporary manger until Frees' slot was filled. The two went into the small office to talk. Several utility and vendors' bills were on the desk, lying atop file folders. The two stood before the desk, looking at each other.

"Just making sure everything is up to date," he said, referring to the paperwork. He lowered his head. "But Don was always on top of stuff like that."

"Good guy, huh?" Hollis looked from the desk to the young man.

"Yeah, he was okay for an old dude."

Hollis asked, "Had there been trouble lately? You know, somebody coming in getting all rowdy and Frees had to show him the door?"

"This cop asked me that. But no, Don was the kind of guy who could make you listen, you know? I mean, this store sponsored a little league team. He did that costume thing to reach out, you know? I mean, he liked to do it, him and Blanca. But he was real, man."

Hollis gave an understanding nod.

13

***

By four he was sitting in the office of Blanca Dunstler. She'd been in the warrior woman costume in the video.

"This is about the terrible misfortune that happened to the lovely Willow, eh, friend Hollis?" She'd risen from behind her desk when he was ushered in. She indicated a comfortable chair. He'd been at the window, looking out through the blinds. He turned and sat down. She also sat again, interlacing her long fingers together on the desktop. A window overlooking the Silver Lake Reservoir was behind her.

"Yes. I appreciate you taking the time to see me, Ms. Dunstler." He sat, crossing his legs and placing his hat on his knee. "Related to her matter, I have good news. Mickey Stratham's come out of his surgery and right about now my good buddy Maynard Regus of the LAPD should be getting his statement." Hollis was lying.

The big woman's shoulders and fingers tightened and momentarily her face clouded, but then cleared. "Really? Well, I wish him God's speed."

Hollis made a non-committal sound. "There are five Chicken Delight franchises you run, isn't that right?"

A tight smile. "Yes, that is so."

"Donald Frees was one of your managers. And you killed him and Willow Ahn. Lonely deaths."

"You need to remove yourself from my presence, jackanape." She swelled.

Hollis remained calm. "So you can run, Blanca? I know Frees had a few conversations with a deputy DA, 'cause I called over there. He'd alleged some irregularities in receipts between what his store turned in and what had been reported to corporate. Irregularities going back several months. He probably talked to you about it first, but you must have stonewalled him. He was scheduled to come in to talk to the DA."

Her shoulders deflated.

"Let me try this out on you. I know you dropped in on Willow and a few others who'd taken Alister Clemments to a bar called the White Palace in West Hollywood after his book signing." The Book Soup's assistant manager hadn't gone out with them, but had overheard which bar they were going to. The tattooed waitress there remembered the group because of Clemments, and a "funny talking, weightlifter broad" who'd joined them when Hollis had shown her Dunstler's photo printout among the others.

"Listen, this...this merely got out of hand," Dunstler said. "But I can add weight to your purse, good sir."

"I probably have a price, Blanca. But my clients paid me the magnificent sum of five hundred dollars they could scrape together to find out who killed their friend. I get that you murdered Frees and made it look like a robbery. Could be you tried to buy him off first like with me. From what I've gathered, he was a straight shooter. He stumbled on the double accounting, only wasn't sure who it was. He came to you as he should have, since you're the one in charge."

Hollis cut his hand through the air. "And Stratham, well, he's a prick. I'm guessing he sold you a gun under the counter, and knew from the *Voice* online story the caliber of the bullet that killed Frees. He's a bottom feeder, so he probably tried to blackmail you."

She unhinged her fingers.

"You liked to dress up, Blanca. You didn't need to work the Boulevard, but I understand from Linda Brenner you dug being in costume at the fantasy and comic book conventions. Frees had introduced you to her and Eva. You'd promised to put up some dough at one point but insisted on being in the production." He paused, frowning. "That's it, you liked Willow too. You came by the bar 'cause you were getting ready to run and wanted Willow to be with you."

She rose. "Are you done?"

"Just as soon as I make a call." Hollis got up too.

Blanca Dunstler smiled and tipped the desk over at Hollis. He stepped back out of the way as she lunged to a nearby closet. She got the door open, revealing her warrior woman costume, and drew her broadsword.

"You don't know what love is, varlet."

"Are you fuckin' kidding me, lady?"

Wielding the sword in her business suit, she chopped it overhand at Hollis, cleaving the thing into the chair as he dove aside. He'd been stabbed in the side once on a case. He didn't want to get skewered again. And this time, he didn't have his gun with him.

She got her weapon loose and came at him again, tears in her eyes. "She rebuffed my entreaty at my abode later that eve." She stalked toward him, Hollis getting around the other side of the desk, the window at his back. "Though I did seek to entice her with the knowledge of the riches I'd accumulated."

He could see in the closet a dagger on the costume in its scabbard and something else. He kicked a corner of the desk, shoving in into Dunstler. He got to the closet and threw one of the free weight disks sitting on the floor. She smiled wickedly as she batted the first one aside with a swipe of her sword. But the second one he aimed, the ten pounder, knocked her upside her head and she dropped to the floor heavily.

"Don't try it," he warned her. Sword in hand, tip to her chest, Hollis stood over Dunstler flat on the floor, crimson leaking from her temple.

***

"Darling," Kristy Simons murmured to Hollis in the dark. They lay entwined in bed, her lover dozing.

"Yes, baby doll."

"How'd you know to call the DA's office?"

"You asking for the piece Harper is writing, or your own edification, my sweet?"

She reached below his navel.

"Since you put it that way." They kissed briefly. "When I went to talk to the Chicken Delight employees, I saw a phone bill on the interim manager's desk. I recognized the main number listed on it to the DA's office."

"Clever fellow aren't you?"

"Hmmmm." Hollis began to doze again. "I figure Dunstler bought the gun from Stratham in anticipation of skipping town with her ill-gotten gains. But needed to hang around for Frees' funeral so she didn't raise suspicions."

Silence then, "Nate?"

"Yes?"

"How about a picture of you with some of the costume

characters for the article?"

He groaned.

A KING'S GAME

by

Phillip Drayer Duncan

"Candy?" James asked.

"Yeah," Nate Hollis replied. "You'll get candy real soon, James."

"You shouldn't lie to him," Barton said.

Hollis shot him a meaningful glare but didn't reply. Billy Barton was a bounty hunter. A small time guy from a small town in the Midwest. His job normally consisted of chasing cattle thieves and low-lifes with warrants. In Angeltown he was out of his element.

They'd only met a few nights before. Barton had approached Hollis and told him he'd been hired by some corporate exec to find a missing nephew. The man had a mental disorder and a tendency to run away. He'd gone missing from a small town outside of Denver and Barton had tracked him as far as Los Angeles. But once in the city, the trail had gone cold. That was where Hollis came in. Apparently the big time corporate goon had gotten his name from somewhere.

Hollis didn't like working with strangers. He especially didn't like to work with bounty hunters, with the exception of his friend and sometime enemy, Irma "Deuce" Deucett. But the money had been right and though he wouldn't admit it, he knew a mentally unstable man wouldn't last long in Los Angeles. Too many demons roamed the streets of Angeltown.

Hollis had reluctantly agreed.

It was a good thing, too. James hadn't been terribly hard to find, but that was only because the P.I. knew where to look. Barton the bounty hunter would have been lost on his own. When they found James in a local shelter, the volunteer staff told them they thought he was just another burnout.

"Home?" James asked.

"We're taking you home," Hollis said, and looked over his shoulder to flash James a grin in the back seat. He glanced toward Barton. "That's not a lie, is it?"

The bounty hunter shrugged and pointed at the address on the gate. "This is it."

"No kidding," Hollis replied. "I told you I knew the neighborhood."

"Want a trophy? The mighty P.I. finds an address. Woohoo."

Hollis chuckled. Despite their differences, Barton wasn't too bad of a guy. They'd managed to find James, anyway.

They were in an upscale, gated neighborhood in Hidden Hills. Not the richest place in L.A., but wealthy enough. There was a "For Sale" sign beside the gate. *These corporate types*, Hollis thought, *they have more money than they know what to do with*. The uncle was probably selling this house just to buy another down the road.

They got James out of the car and approached the door. Barton hit the doorbell and they waited.

After a few moments the door opened and a young black man in an expensive suit invited them in. He shook Barton's hand, then turned to Hollis. "You must be Nate Hollis. It's a pleasure to meet you. I'm Terrell."

Hollis offered his hand and met a firm grip. "Damn, man. You trying to break my hand off?"

"Sorry," he said as color flushed his cheeks. "I sometimes get a little overzealous. I've heard about you. You're a real hero in the streets. You as good as they say?"

"Were you a hoopster, or did you play a real sport?" Hollis asked.

"What?" he replied, his surprise evident. "Football. How'd you know?"

"Saw your ring," Hollis replied, feeling a bit cocky. The P.I. part of him would have liked to have said he noticed the ring straight away, but the truth of it was he'd felt it squeeze his hand.

"State championship wasn't it?"

"It is. I played a bit of ball, back in the day."

"Yeah, me too," Barton said. "Are we going to stand here and measure each other's man bits, or we going to get James to his Uncle?"

"Candy?" James asked.

"Right," Terrell said. "Follow me."

It wasn't the nicest house any of Hollis's clients had ever owned, but it was way fancier than anything he could afford.

Terrell led them directly to a study down the hall.

It was dimly lit and the walls were lined with shelves filled with old books he doubted anyone had ever read. There were a few antique parlor chairs to entertain guests and a giant mahogany desk near the back of the room.

Two large men stood on either side of the desk in suits every bit as expensive as Terrell's. They didn't seem as friendly, though. One was Hispanic and his head was shaved to display a nasty scar on the top of his skull. The other was white and had an equally nasty scar above one eye. Both men looked out of place in their expensive suits. Hollis knew the type, bruisers.

The client himself was an older white man. Hollis didn't know his first name. He was one of those important types who only went by his surname. Mr. Luther.

He was sitting behind the desk but rose as they entered the room. Luther headed straight to James and hugged him. "My nephew." When he released James he turned back to the others, giving both Hollis and Barton a once over. "You found him. I can't believe it. You actually did it."

"It was our job," Barton replied.

"And we're really good at it," Hollis said. "Well, I am, at least."

"You did great work," he said. "Please, come, have a seat. Don't mind my bodyguards. Toro and Ox are both gentlemen."

Hollis didn't bother sharing his thoughts on the matter.

He ushered them toward the chairs and Hollis reluctantly took a seat. He didn't like hanging out with rich people. He would have preferred to get paid and go, but knew it would be better in the long term to not offend the client. Helping out a powerful business man on a legitimate job had its perks. It could get him more work in the future.

"Can I offer you gentlemen a drink?" he asked. "I have scotch, bourbon, brandy."

"I'll take a bourbon," Hollis said.

"Same," Barton replied.

As Mr. Luther poured the drinks he said, "I was just sitting here admiring my new toy and wondering if you gentlemen were having any luck." He offered them each a glass filled with amber liquid and stepped back to pour one for himself. "Are either of you gentlemen interested in firearms?"

"I'm mostly interested in avoiding being shot by them," Hollis said.

Barton shrugged. "I'm a country boy. Of course I'm into firearms."

Mr. Luther stepped back over to his desk and picked up a sleek, gold-plated handgun. Hollis wasn't an expert on firearms, but it was the classic 1911 model and therefore most likely a .45. Personally he wasn't into flashy weapons, but he had to admit it was one of the nicest guns he'd ever seen.

Mr. Luther passed it to Barton, who gave it a careful inspection. "It's extraordinary."

"A custom job," Mr. Luther said. "You don't even want to know what it cost."

"No, I don't," Barton said. "It's beautiful, though."

Barton handed the gun to Hollis, and despite his disinterest, he took it and looked it over just as Barton had. He *really* didn't want to offend a client who could afford a toy like that.

"Check out the sights," Mr. Luther said.

Hollis wrapped his hand around the handle and aimed toward the bookcase. He couldn't argue with the weight or balance. It was one hell of a firearm.

He handed it back to the smiling Mr. Luther, who drew a full clip from his pocket and slid it into the gun. He worked the slide and chambered a round. Without another word he walked over to James, put the gun to his head, and pulled the trigger.

The gun roared. Blood sprayed the nearby bookcase. James slumped over, dead, a large crater in the side of his head.

Hollis and Barton both jumped to their feet, but before either could react Mr. Luther trained his gun on them. The two bruisers,

Toro and Ox, drew weapons as well. Only Terrell remained unarmed, and he looked just as surprised.

"I believe that concludes our business," Mr. Luther said. "Good evening."

"You son of a bitch," Barton said, his hand hovering near his own gun.

Hollis was right there with him, but held out a hand and said, "Easy, Barton."

Barton glanced at him, and they both glanced back to Mr. Luther.

"I said good evening, gentlemen," Mr. Luther said.

"I believe that's our cue to leave," Hollis said.

As they eased their way toward the door Mr. Luther said, "Oh, and gentlemen, do keep this to yourselves. Your fingerprints are on the murder weapon, after all."

The P.I. and the bounty hunter headed toward the door.

***

Hollis kicked in the dingy motel door and charged inside. As he'd hoped, he caught the bounty hunter with his pants down, quite literally. Barton had been sitting on the bed flipping through the latest issue of *Big Jugs*. When the door crashed in he threw the mag aside and dove for his gun. Hollis jumped on the bed, caught a bounce, and dove for the bounty hunter, all while being thankful he'd kicked the door in before Barton had gotten into the stroke of things.

He crashed into Barton just as his gun cleared his holster. The two hit the ground and struggled for control of both the gun and each other. Neither seemed to get the immediate upper hand, but Hollis got the impression the corn-fed country boy might have some strength on him. He gave up on fighting for the gun and punched Barton in the nose. He didn't have a good angle from the floor so he wasn't able to get a good swing, but it surely had to sting.

Barton replied by thumping a fat knuckle in the center of Hollis's forehead. In return, Hollis attempted to jab him in the eye. Barton evaded and bit Hollis on the hand.

"Ow! What the hell, Barton? Biting? Really?"

"Whatever it takes! You're trying to kill me!"

"I'm not trying to kill you, you damn fool!"

"Then why are we beating the shit out of each other?" Barton asked as he scooched away and rested his back against the nearest bed.

"You set me up," Hollis said.

Both men eyed the gun lying on the floor between them, but neither made a move on it.

"I didn't set you up."

"Bullshit. There never was a Mr. Luther and there never was a nephew. I've searched and searched. They don't exist. Even the home was a fake. The realtor had it furnished for an open house."

"Then who were they?"

"You tell me. You're the one that tracked James to Angeltown and dragged me into this mess."

"True, but I didn't know what was going to happen. Why do you think I'm still in town? I want to find that prick."

"I'm not buying that," Hollis said, but before he could continue the motel phone rang.

They both glanced at it and Barton said, "See what you've done, city boy. Noise complaint, no doubt."

"Whatever," Hollis said as he grabbed the phone.

He was about to tell the manager on the other end he'd tripped over the bed and sorry for the noise, but before he could the voice on the other end said, "Is this Billy or Nathaniel?"

"Who do you think you're calling Nathaniel?"

"Would you prefer Nate?"

"It's Hollis," he said as he recognized the voice of Mr. Luther. "How the hell did you know I was here?"

"I've been waiting for the two of you to get together again. Waiting to see if the P.I. could track down the bounty hunter. Tell me how you did it."

"Piss off," Hollis replied.

Mr. Luther chuckled. "Put me on speaker phone, please."

"This is a motel phone, jackass. It doesn't have speaker."

"Oh right," he replied. "Hold on a moment. I'll call you right back."

The phone clicked over as he hung up. Hollis stared at the receiver.

"Who was it?" Barton asked.

"Mr. Luther."

"Shit. What did he want?"

"I don't know. He said he'd call right back. Eccentric bastard."

Hollis' cell phone rang. It was an unknown number. He glanced at Barton and said, "This is really starting to freak me out."

Barton nodded and scooped his gun up from the floor.

Hollis answered and put it in on speaker.

"Am I on speaker now?" Mr. Luther asked.

"You are," Hollis replied.

"Ah, Nathaniel Hollis," he said. "The rough and tumble private investigator who just wants answers for dearest dad's death. And Billy Barton, the broken-hearted bounty hunter. Another man just looking for answers."

Hollis and Barton shared a look. Mr. Luther knew too much.

"Who are you really?" Hollis asked. "Mr. Luther is a fake name. I know that much."

He fell into another fit of laughter. "I've been known by many names, but my favorite is King. You can call me that."

"I think I'd rather call you asshole," Barton replied.

"What do you want?" Hollis asked.

"I want you to come find me," King replied. "I want to see if you little pawns are as good as your reputations."

"That would be an absolute pleasure," Barton replied.

"Good. But don't keep me waiting long. I might decide to hand this gun over to the police with an anonymous tip about a P.I. and a bounty hunter I saw kill a poor disabled man."

The call ended.

"Weird," Barton said.

"Something isn't right," Hollis said. "Why would he call us and tell us to come find him?"

Barton shrugged. "When we do, can we kick his teeth in?"

"I'm game," Hollis replied. "That's the least he deserves for what he did to James."

"Have any ideas where to start looking?"

"I say we start with Terrell Davis."

"The doorman?"

"Yeah," Hollis replied. "We know something about him. He

played football. And he's got a high school state championship ring."

"Yeah, but what state?"

"Hopefully California. That will make things easier. We can guess his age within a few years and check records for each division, find the winners within that time frame, and then crosscheck the names."

"How the hell are we going to do all of that?"

"Internet," Hollis replied. "How else? You don't use Google when you're chasing cows?"

Barton snickered but didn't reply.

"Also, I may have access to sites restricted to investigators and lawyers," Hollis replied. "You know, for investigating things."

***

It took a few hours and a couple of cups of coffee, but eventually Hollis found what he was looking for. Terrell Davis had gone to Long Beach Polytechnic High School. He graduated in '98 with a state championship in division one.

With that intel the search broadened. They couldn't find a current address for Terrell himself, but they did dig up an address for his parents. They would surely have an address for their son.

It was a start.

***

The house was in Hyde Park and sat wedged in a row on a busy street. A late '90s Blazer sat in the driveway. A couple of pieces of siding had fallen off the house and the whole thing desperately needed a new coat of paint.

"Our boy didn't come from money," Hollis said.

Barton grunted his agreement and they headed for the door.

As Hollis reached for the doorbell he said, "I should probably do the talking, hillbilly."

"Suits me fine. You city folk are a different breed anyway."

Hollis chuckled and tapped the buzzer. An aging woman opened the door and greeted them. She seemed the right age to be Terrell's mother.

"Mrs. Davis?" Hollis asked.

"Yes?"

"My name is Nate Hollis. We're private investigators and we're working a case. We were hoping we could ask you a few questions about your son."

"Is Terrell in some kind of trouble?" she asked, concern spreading across her face.

"Not at all," Hollis said, working the conversation with practiced ease. "However, an associate of his may be. We're trying to get ahold of Terrell before he gets dragged into the mess, and he may be able to help us clear it up."

"I don't understand."

Hollis offered her a sympathetic smile and said, "Mrs. Davis, I can assure you we have Terrell's best interest at heart. We just want to help him out. He's a great guy."

"You know Terrell?"

"Of course. We both think the world of him."

"Yes ma'am," Barton said. "You raised a great kid."

"Thank you," she said. "I suppose if it's to help Terrell…"

"I assure you it is," Hollis said.

After that Mrs. Davis opened up and started answering questions.

As far as his momma knew, Terrell worked for an accounting firm and held a prestigious position reporting directly to the CEO. She couldn't remember the name of the company but she was sure she had the address somewhere.

***

It looked like an old office building and sat between two similar vacant buildings. If it were open and running, Hollis suspected it wouldn't last long. Then again, it looked like a good place to hide a dirty operation of some kind.

There were a few young men standing up the street in the front. They looked like banger wannabe's out for an afternoon stroll, but they could have been lookouts. Instead of going in through the front, they eased their way toward the building from the back.

He spotted a rear door and watched for a couple of minutes to make sure no one was around. When he felt it was clear, they made their way over. It was an old-style lock, and he was able to pry it open fairly quick with a heavy screw driver.

They went inside.

It appeared to be an old office and at first glance it didn't appear that anyone was home. Hollis moved forward a few steps, hearing voices. He gave Barton a wave and they headed in a different direction. He wasn't ready to be caught just yet. He wanted to check things out first.

The front side of the building was a maze of cubicles, and despite each desk having a monitor and phone, there was no one working on them. They moved on.

Hollis thought he heard a faint noise from a nearby room, and almost passed, but stopped again. The sound he heard was crying.

He motioned to Barton and drew his gun just in case. Barton did the same. Hollis turned the knob and was met with darkness, but he knew the cry for what it was then. It was the sob of a child... no he realized, several.

He let his hand fumble around on the wall until he felt a light switch and flicked it on.

Chained together, one by one and sitting on the floor were a number of children. They were of various races but they were young and they were all frightened.

"We've got to get them out of here," Barton said.

Hollis nodded.

Before they could, a sound from behind brought Hollis around and he realized an Asian man was standing in the hall behind him. They stared at each other in equal surprise for a few moments, then the Asian man screamed and started for his gun. Hollis already had his at the ready, so instead the thug took to running for cover instead.

"Damn," Hollis said. "We've got trouble."

From down the hall a swarm of Asian gang bangers poured around the corner with guns ready.

Hollis and Barton had no choice but to make a run for it. They headed back into the main office area and dove for cover behind a metal desk as the gunfire started. Holes punched through the wood around them. After a few moments it died off and Barton shouted, "I don't think this is an accounting firm."

"No kidding," Hollis replied, noting the sarcasm.

Hollis wasn't sure what gang they were a part of -- it could have been the ABZ or the EFCC. Hell, as far as he knew they could have been Tiny Rascals. Maybe they weren't associated with a gang at all. They looked like bangers, though, and they were rocking full auto submachine guns.

"What do you think they're up to in here?" Barton asked.

"Child sex trafficking, if I had to guess," Hollis replied. "Terrell's momma sent us here. Ask her."

"You think she knew?"

"Or this is really where her son worked. It wouldn't surprise me if this is the kind of shit King is into."

Hollis fired a few rounds over the desk and tucked back down into cover. He didn't always carry a gun, but given the strange circumstances, he'd thought it might be useful. He really wished he had a bazooka.

"So, we have a plan?" Barton asked. "Or are we just going with the good ole try not to die? If any of these pricks could shoot straight we'd be dead already."

"Maybe they'll run out of bullets," Hollis offered. There were at least four shooters he'd seen, but guessed there were more. They were outgunned and he didn't have any clever tricks up his sleeve – well, one.

"See that fire extinguisher nearer to you?" Hollis said.

"Cover me," Barton said.

Before Hollis could ask why, Barton dove for the desk next to them. Gunfire traced his movement, but they couldn't get the bead on him. Hollis stuck his gun over the desk and fired off a few rounds, forcing their assailants back under cover.

Barton moved to the wall and ripped off the fire extinguisher, then hurled it across the room at the thugs. Hollis was impressed with the man's strength and thought himself lucky their earlier scuffle hadn't gone a different way. The country boy was strong.

Barton made his way back and said, "When I hit the extinguisher, gun 'em down!" Without waiting for a reply Barton rose and shot the fire extinguisher. A white cloud dispersed among the shooters, and for a moment they stopped firing.

Hollis and Barton, on the other hand, released a salvo of rounds. He didn't see any of their bullets strike, but there were at least a few yelps of pain.

When the smoke finally cleared the shooters were out of sight, but there was a trail of blood where they fled.

Hollis and Barton eased their way out of cover and headed back for the children. They didn't meet any resistance, but were both convinced they weren't out of hot water yet.

The prisoners were chained together but neither end of the chain was tethered. Ensuring that the kids could walk, they started marching them toward the door.

As they reached the nearby side door they'd broken in through, Hollis said, "You know, Barton, that fire extinguisher trick of yours gave me an idea."

"Am I going to like this idea?" Barton replied.

Hollis grinned.

***

Hollis watched as the black smoke rose from the office building. The hail of gunfire had caused a stir in the neighborhood and the police showed up a few minutes after they got the kids out of the building. They'd both been interrogated, but they'd put together a cover story ahead of time. They each separately told the officers they were trying to locate a missing person named Terrell Davis and his mother had given them the address, believing it was the office he worked at. It was close enough to the truth that neither had to worry about messing the story up. And of course, they'd assured both officers that they had no idea how the building had caught on fire. Given the circumstances, their willingness to let the local PD take credit for rescuing the enslaved, the kids' translated statements that the two men had rescued them, and Hollis dropping a certain defense attorney's name, they finally were on their way.

It was time to pay Terrell's mother another visit.

***

When they arrived the Blazer was gone and a For Sale sign was posted in the front yard. Hollis noted the house was being brokered by the same entity in Hidden Hills.

They shared a glance and Hollis waved down a neighbor

moving trash bins.

"Excuse me," he said, "Does the Davis family still live here?"

"The Davis family?" the neighbor replied. "They haven't lived here in years. Not since their son died in that car wreck."

Hollis and Barton shared another look and Hollis asked, "Was their son named Terrell?"

"That sounds right," he said and got back to his trash.

"What the hell?" Barton asked.

Hollis didn't have an answer.

***

Hollis did have an answer about what to do next. The office building which held the kids had to belong to someone. It wouldn't be terribly hard to find out who. He just needed to figure it out before the police did. Once they started down that path, the owner might become a ghost, or worse yet, end up in police custody before Hollis had a chance to ask them a few a questions.

Fortunately, he was able to find what he was looking for and didn't need his computer hacker friend Frag Lawson. The city had records of who owned various properties, and it wasn't exactly confidential information, especially where commercial property was concerned. That property was owned by a false front, but Hollis was able to pierce the veil. The building belonged to an insurance company named Lucky Days Insurance. Unfortunately, it went out of business a year back. It seemed to be a dead end.

Hollis kept searching. While the official website was down, it was still listed on a number of business review sites. It was listed as closed, but they still had the company's information, including the former owner's name. Damien White.

Again Hollis searched, this time for information on Mr. White, but found nothing. He placed another call to the city and found out that there was another property he was listed as the owner of.

"You know," Barton said as they got ready. "After our last experience, I can't help thinking we're going to find ourselves walking into a bear trap. We need to gear up. I need ammo. And if you have machine guns lying around, that would be nice. Or a bazooka."

"I don't have a bazooka," Hollis said. "But I do have something just as good."

"What's that?"

"A Deuce," Hollis replied as he dialed another number.

***

They met Irma Deuce a few blocks from the address.

"Damn," Barton said as they pulled up. "You weren't kidding. Tough looking gal."

Deuce gave the two a hard look as they approached. Like Barton, Irma Deuce was a bounty hunter. She was also a bodybuilder and a hell of a lot tougher than most of the men Hollis knew.

Hollis supposed they were friends, but at times they were known to bump heads, and he wouldn't go so far as to say he trusted her completely. Still, he knew he could count on her in a pinch, and the feeling was mutual.

"Deuce," he said as they approached.

"Hollis," she replied, then turned toward Barton. "This your bounty hunter? Doesn't look like much."

"I got it where it counts," Barton replied.

"I guess we'll see."

"You can see anything you'd like, ma'am."

Deuce's eyes hardened, but before she could reply Hollis stepped in. "All right you two. We got work to do. You can measure your dicks later. And Barton, fair warning, hers is bigger."

"Damn," Barton said. "You just ruined the image in my head."

Hollis ignored him and instead asked Deuce, "Did you bring the goods?"

"Of course," she replied, leading them around to her trunk.

"Sweet baby Jesus," Barton said as she showed them what goodies she'd brought. "Marry me, Deuce."

He reached for a pistol grip shotgun and Deuce said, "If you want to keep that hand…"

Barton paused.

"The semi-auto is my baby," she said as she removed it from

the trunk. "You boys get the pumps."

Barton didn't argue and removed one of the pump-action shotguns. In addition to those she'd brought spare handguns, a boatload of ammo, and bulletproof vests.

"So what are we expecting?" Deuce asked as she loaded shells into her shotgun.

"The unexpected," Hollis replied.

"Helpful," she replied. "Just make sure I get paid."

"Only if we don't end up dead."

***

It was a rather large warehouse, and it appeared to be just as abandoned as the converted suites of offices. Somehow he doubted it. Surrounding the place was a fair amount of shrubbery, bushes, and trees, which offered just the concealment they needed to work their way close unseen.

They crept around to the back where they found a number of guards standing around silently watching for trespassers.

"Bingo," Hollis whispered.

"Two Uzi's and a Tech Nine," Barton said. "Certainly seems like it might be the right place. And they're Asian. Same gang as before?"

"Not sure," Hollis said. "Let's see if we can find an easier way in."

They worked their way back through the landscape and continued creeping until they found a side door guarded by only one man.

"Looks like this is our best entry point," Hollis said.

"Yup," Barton replied. "Got it."

Barton disappeared among the bushes.

"What's the fool doing?" Deuce asked.

Hollis shrugged.

Barton went up the row of shrubs a short way then stepped out and crossed over to the side of the building. The guard faced forward, so Barton eased his way toward him from the side. As he closed the distance between them he said, "Hey bud, you got a light?"

The guard jumped in surprise. Hollis imagined he was only

more surprised when Barton pelted him between the eyes with the butt of his shotgun. The guard went down. Barton scooped up the automatic weapon, slung the strap over his shoulder, and turned to wave at Hollis.

"Show off," Deuce said as she and Hollis stepped out of their hiding spot.

"Crazy ass country folk," Hollis replied.

Together they crept into the warehouse. Hollis took point, which was fine with the others. None of them knew where they were going.

They moved past a number of rooms and were forced into hiding a few times as people walked by.

Hollis held up his hand for them to stop again when he heard voices up ahead. He couldn't make out what was said, but it sounded like two men talking. He started forward again and realized the voices were coming from within an open door down the hall. As he moved closer, he could finally make out the conversation.

"What are we going to do?" one asked.

"Set up shop somewhere else. What else?"

"I know, but it's still a big loss. At least the coke didn't get hit."

"Of course it's a big loss. Those sniveling brats were worth a ton of money, but we'll just have to get more."

"How'd they even find it?"

"I don't know. I've heard of this Hollis. I'll tell you one thing, if he was here I'd skin that prick."

"Here I am," Hollis said as he entered the room and leveled his shotgun at the two men. He couldn't help himself.

There were two of them. One wore an expensive business suit while the other wore tailored slacks and a Hawaiian shirt. Both were getting up in age. Behind them, four Asian women in their underwear were separating, weighing, and bagging a substantial mountain of processed cocaine. It reminded Hollis of a scene from *Scarface*.

The one in the suit said, "How the hell did you get in here? And who the hell are you?" He had a gun in his hand as did the other man.

"Hollis, P.I., at your service. Where the hell is King?"

"Who's King?"

There was a moment of silence as they all stared at one another. Hollis had a sneaking suspicion they hadn't come to the right place – or rather had been led here. But clearly they'd been talking about the child slavery ring. Was King involved with it somehow?

"Let's not get ahead of ourselves," Barton said. "Why don't we start by having each of you set your guns on the floor?"

"I'm going to have to agree with the hillbilly," Deuce said. "One at a time, set your pieces on the ground."

Business suit and Hawaiian Shirt placed their firearms on the floor. The women became motionless. Hollis and Deuce kept their guns trained on them while Barton stepped forward to collect.

"I'm not sure what you're hoping to gain here," Business Suit said, "but you've made a terrible mistake."

"Is that right?" Hollis said. "Are you Damien White?"

"Yes, and yes," he replied and raised his hand to reveal a small device. "This is a remote panic button. Welcome to the future, my friends. Every armed man on the property knows I'm in trouble."

"You're bluffing," Deuce said.

"I assure you I'm not. Did the Ghost send you?"

"The Ghost?" Hollis said. The pieces were starting to come together.

"A competitor. For the past month or so he's been a real thorn in my side. Why do you think I have all of the guards?"

Hollis and Barton shared a look. Hollis said, "Your Ghost is the one we're trying to find. Do you know what he looks like?"

"No. I don't know much about him."

"Tell us what you do know."

"Why?"

"Because we're going to put him out of business."

"And I suppose you want me to let you walk on out of here? I'm afraid that's not an option."

Several armed Asian men appeared at the door. Deuce leveled her shotgun at them. It was a standoff.

"You see," Damien said. "You're quite stuck."

Hollis showed his phone. It was on. He said clearly, "My name is Nate Hollis and I'm a licensed private investigator. I'm at a location where there's a mountain of cocaine that would give Tony Montana a hard-on. I'm also surrounded by a number of thugs and their would-be kingpins. All armed of course."

"Seriously?" the dispatcher replied. He sounded young. "Is this a joke?"

"You gonna ping my phone or not?"

"Uh, yeah, I mean if you're serious."

Hollis glared grimly at Damien White, then turned back to the thugs in the doorway.

"Hey, Deuce," he said, still looking at the thugs. "What do they call it when you get arrested with a mountain of coke and fully automatic weapons?"

"You know, I can't think of the legal slang, but I believe the term is *screwed*."

The thugs shifted nervously and a few started backing away from the door.

"Wait," Hollis said. "If you just bail they'll hunt you down. And I know your type, you'll all squeal on each other. The police are only interested in the big dogs. Give them up and they won't give a shit about you cats."

"We give them up, they don't come after us?" One of them asked.

"That's my guess," Hollis said. "Either way, it's your safest bet."

They looked at each other and began speaking in an Asian dialect. Hollis didn't know which and couldn't understand a word of it.

Almost simultaneously, the thugs dropped their guns to the floor and entered the room. Hollis and company stood aside while they tied their bosses to their chairs.

"Do you know who I am?" Hawaiian shirt said.

Damien White pleaded as well. "You all work for me. I'll give you raises."

It didn't matter. The thugs had only one loyalty and it was to themselves individually.

When they finished, they left the room without another word.

"You'll pay for this, Hollis," White said.

"Yeah, yeah," Hollis replied as they too, headed for the door.

***

Hollis munched on his burrito in silence and thought the situation over.

"What next?" Barton said, echoing his own thoughts. Barton took a bite out of a taco and said, "We need a plan."

"Don't talk with your mouth full. Here in the civilized world it's considered poor manners."

"If you call this civilized, I'm not too worried about it."

"Can't argue with that," Deuce said. "But the hillbilly is right. This is a weird situation you're in. If you don't have any other leads I need to get back to my own work."

"As Business Suit noted," Hollis said, pausing to reaffirm his suspicions, "we've been used to take out some of the competition."

Barton nodded. "But why? King has goons of his own. Anyone who can afford a golden .45 can afford a few henchmen to dirty work."

Hollis nodded. "This is a game to him. Moving the pieces about."

Barton snorted. "I don't know, none of this really makes sense."

Hollis started to take another bite of his burrito but paused. Instead, he said, "Wait, what did you just say?"

"That none of this really makes sense."

"No," Hollis said, his eyes widening. "The gun! That's it!"

Barton's eyes lit up as well, catching Hollis's meaning.

Hollis grinned. "King said the gun was a custom job, and it was brand new. If any of that had been true, someone crafted it recently. There would be a record. It wasn't like just anyone could have made it. It would have been a professional gunsmith. Hell, they probably would have even put a picture of it on their website.

***

Despite the fact California had some of the strictest gun laws in the country, Hollis was surprised by how many custom firearms dealers there were in the state. But whittling it down to high-end firearms wasn't terribly hard, and in short order he found exactly what he was looking for.

"Rick's Custom Firearms," he read aloud, then cast a grin toward Barton. "Check this out."

Barton peered over Hollis's shoulder. There was a picture of the gold plated 1911 on the website. It was listed as Rick's most recent creation. Of course, the website wouldn't have buyer information posted.

Hollis toyed with the idea of calling the place and seeing if he could squeeze out a name, but he doubted they'd give it up, no matter how smooth he could be. High-end clientele always wanted to be discreet, and Hollis had a feeling that was especially true in the gun business.

He reached for his phone and dialed a different number.

She answered on the second ring.

"Monica," he said.

"Hollis," she replied.

Monica Orozco wasn't just another criminal defense attorney, she was a woman who had her own firm which catered to both high-end and low-end clientele. She made her money from helping the Hollywood types, but she had a passion for helping those from the poorer communities as well. She and Hollis had had a thing once...or twice.

"I was wondering if you could help me out," he said. "I need some info."

"Do I look like your personal assistant?"

"Come on, Monica, don't do me like that."

She chuckled. "What do you need?"

"I was wondering if you might engage one of your law enforcement contacts who might be able to look up who purchased a certain kind of gun. I know who made it and I have a description. A collector's piece, not registered."

"Hmm," she said. "I may know a cute DEA agent or two that would be willing to help me out."

"Oh, it's like that, is it?"

"It is," she said. "Give me the info and I'll see what I can find.

You'll owe me one, though."

"You need help on a case you let me know."

"Not sure it's a case I'll want your help with, handsome. We'll see."

Hollis provided her the information and ended the phone call.

***

Hollis was still waiting to hear back from Monica when the call came. Assuming it was her, he didn't even bother to look at the caller ID when he answered.

It was Hollis' grandfather, Obediah "Clutch" Hollis. A former professional football player in his younger days, Clutch had turned bar owner in his later years. He ran an old school establishment called the Hideaway, and he was the closest family Hollis had left. As much as Hollis wanted to find out who killed his dad, Clutch wanted to find out who killed his son.

"Nate," he said. "You in some kind of trouble again?"

"Why?"

"Because there're a couple of ruffians dressed in suits in my bar. I don't like men in suits in my bar."

"Is one of them a Chicano with a scar on his bald head?"

"Yeah. Friends of yours?"

Hollis checked his watch. It was still early. "Are you the only one in the bar?"

"Yeah. Why?"

"I'm on my way."

***

The Hideaway was empty and the doors were unlocked. Clutch was gone. The only logical explanation was he'd been taken. There were no signs of a struggle, though. Perhaps they hadn't hurt him yet.

He was about to curse when his phone rang. It was an unknown number. He answered.

"Hello, Nathaniel," King's voice said. "No, I'm sorry, it's Hollis, right?"

"You took Clutch."

"I did," he said. It was so nonchalant it made Hollis want to scream. "I thought you might need a little encouragement. I can see you're making progress, but you haven't found me yet."

"Oh, I'll find you," Hollis said, gritting his teeth. "Don't worry about that. I'm coming."

"Good," he said. "Hurry along. Don't dilly dally."

The phone call ended and Hollis said, "He's taken Clutch."

Bastard," Deuce replied. She and Hollis might not have been best friends, but she adored the old man too. It had just become personal for her as well. "What are we going to do?"

Before Hollis could answer, his phone rang again. This time it *was* Monica.

She told him that the gun had been made for an Andrew Goldsmith. She didn't just get a name, but an address too. Hollis thanked her but ended the call before she could ask what was wrong. She must have heard it in his voice. He didn't want to explain.

He turned to the others and said, "Let's go."

"Woah," Barton said. "I thought you wanted to play this smart. Maybe see what we can find out about this guy beforehand?"

"That was before they took Clutch."

"Look, I get it. He's your grandfather. I'd be pissed too. But it would be foolish to go charging in there unprepared. Are you sure this is how you want to play it?"

"I thought you liked foolish, country boy."

"Fair point," Barton said as he started forward as well. "I just wish we had a bazooka."

***

It was in Bel Air, which Barton found quite humorous. Hollis, on the other hand, was annoyed he had to listen to Barton sing the Fresh Prince song for the whole drive. It would be stuck in his head for weeks.

To make matters worse, as Barton took his turn with the binoculars he sang, "Moving on up."

"Are you really quoting the theme song from "The Jefferson's" right now?" Deuce asked.

"Yes ma'am," Barton replied. "Out in the country the newest TV we get is thirty years old. So no spoilers, please."

Deuce turned to Hollis. "I can't tell if he's messing with me or not."

Hollis smiled.

"What's the plan?" Barton asked.

"It's probably best if we stick together," Hollis said. "We don't know how many goons we're up against. Finding Clutch is our priority."

"Understood," Barton said. "We ready to do this thing, or what?"

***

The lights were on but the house was quiet. They met no resistance as they made their approach. Still, they decided to play it safe and headed for a side door.

Hollis reached for the knob and was surprised to find it unlocked.

"Creepy," Deuce said as Hollis opened it.

"You ever get the feeling they're expecting us?" Barton asked. "Hell, they should have sent us a Facebook invitation."

"You use Facebook?" Deuce asked.

"Don't everyone?"

"Quiet, you two," Hollis said.

They moved into the house. Much to his surprise, they weren't immediately riddled with bullets.

"All right," Hollis whispered. "You two are the bounty hunters. Where do you think they hid him?"

"Basement," Deuce replied.

"Pool," Barton said. As they both gave him a skeptical look he said, "I like to think I'd be a really fun kidnapper."

They continued staring.

"I don't know," he said. "Where I'm from bounty hunting don't usually involve hunting people who've been kidnapped. Kidnappers, maybe. But not kidnappees."

"Shh," Hollis said. "Someone's coming."

Hollis and Barton dove behind a nearby couch. Deuce, who at

the moment was probably the smarter of the three, opened a nearby door and stepped inside.

A few moments later they heard a pair of feet walk past the couch. They came to a stop and one of the voices said, "Has anyone found that crafty old bastard yet?"

Silence.

"Yeah, well he needs to be found so we can set the ambushes back up."

Silence.

"I know he hurt two of the guys, but the boss said only to kill him if we absolutely have to. He wants him alive until the P.I. and the bounty hunter are dead."

Silence.

"All right, let me know when they find him."

They started walking again, and once they were past his hiding spot Hollis stepped out of cover. He drilled the first in the back of the head with the butt of his shotgun. Barton did the same to the other. Both hit the ground.

"Damn, sounds like your grandfather is a tough old bastard," Barton said.

"He is," Hollis replied, pointing at the unconscious men. "Look at these guys. Business suits. They aren't bangers."

Barton nodded. "Professionals maybe."

"They can't be too good," Deuce said as she stepped out of her hiding place. "You two knocked them out."

"We have to find Clutch," Hollis said, ignoring the insult. "That old fool is likely to get himself killed."

"I heard," she replied. "Time to take off the kid gloves?"

"You know it," Hollis replied. "We need to try to take them down without too much noise, but we're going to rip every inch of this place apart until we find him."

***

They didn't actually rip the house apart, but they were steadily working through the goons. Their luck had held up pretty well. They'd managed to knock out two more sets of thugs and were still working their way through the house when they came around a corner and found themselves face to face with a group of five.

Hollis smashed the butt of his gun into the face of one and then attempted to tackle the whole pile. It wasn't the best strategy, but it kept them from opening fire. One crawled on top of Hollis and tried to pin him down. Barton kicked him in the ribs and bashed his gun into the face of another. Deuce kicked a man between the legs and pelted him in the head with her shotgun as well.

Hollis found himself on top of one goon who managed to catch him with a solid punch to the jaw. Hollis responded by breaking the guy's nose with a stiff right.

One of the first class thugs trained a gun on Barton, but Deuce slapped it aside just as the weapon went off, leaving a hole in the wall instead of Barton.

Hollis's ears rang from the gun's rapport. Everyone in the house would have heard it. They'd lost the element of surprise.

Deuce grabbed the shooter by the throat and slammed him through the drywall, and even snapped a stud within. Another of the assailants tackled her around the waist and tried to drive her to the ground. At the gym Deuce never cheated on leg day. She wasn't going down.

More enemies charged around the corner but didn't open fire. They were probably worried about shooting their allies, Hollis thought. Two holstered their weapons and charged into the fray. One stayed behind and watched.

One of the newcomers slipped in behind Barton and attempted to stick him in a half-Nelson while he traded blows with another. Barton surged forward and planted a steel toe in the shin of the one in front. Then he jerked his head back and slammed it into the nose of the one behind.

Hollis was still on the ground and caught up in something of a wrestling match against two opponents. One attempted to restrain his wrists to stop Hollis from punching him in the face.

The other managed to gain his feet and kicked Hollis in the thigh. It would leave a wicked bruise but no real damage. Hollis kicked back in reply. He didn't have the best angle, but still managed to make the man stumble slightly and turn, giving Hollis the shot he wanted. He drew his foot back and fired it forward into the side of the man's kneecap. There was a pop, followed by a scream, and he went down.

Hollis turned back to the man on the floor and slammed a knee into his crotch. This caused the man to release one of his arms and Hollis elbowed him in the ribs. Both hands free, Hollis climbed on top of him and rained blow after blow into his face.

He might have kept going if not for the feeling of something hard pressed against his forehead. He didn't need to hear the hammer cock back to know what it was. Below him the man he'd pummeled wasn't moving, so he risked a look up.

"End of the line, Hollis," the gunman said. Hollis didn't recognize the man, but it didn't really matter. In his line of work, it was only a matter of time before someone called his number. It didn't really matter who.

He closed his eyes and awaited the boom that would be the last sound he ever heard. Maybe he'd be with his dad. Instead, there was a hollow thump and the pressure of the gun fell away from his head. Hollis opened his eyes to see his assailant fall to the ground. Behind him stood Clutch, and he held a large golden trophy. "Bad guys talk too much."

Hollis sighed as relief flooded his senses. He was alive, but more importantly, Clutch was okay.

"You just gonna sit there, son?"

Hollis rose and clasped his grandfather's shoulder. He glanced back to see how his friends were faring.

Barton had a guy in a sleeper hold and was sending him to dreamland.

Deuce threw another guy into the wall.

Their enemies were all on the floor, either unconscious or pretending to be unconscious.

The group gathered and Barton asked, "Time for a daring escape or a heroic charge?"

"Heroic charge," Hollis said. "But first... Deuce, get Clutch out of here."

"Hey, I'm not some helpless old man," Clutch said as he leaned over to pick up one of the thugs' firearms. "I can hold my own. I got free didn't I?"

"I don't doubt it," Hollis replied. "It's not about that. We may need cover fire to escape, or a getaway driver. We're almost certainly walking into a trap. It won't do any good to get us all caught in it."

"That sounds like a load a bull," Clutch said.

"Deuce," Hollis said, "please get him out of here."

She nodded. "Let's go, Clutch. This isn't our fight anymore."

The old man grudgingly followed Deuce down the hall, but stopped and said, "Don't get yourself killed, Nate. I already lost your father."

***

Around every corner they were prepared to meet the end of a gun barrel, but they met little resistance on their way through the house. Just a few stragglers they took down easily enough. The first two they got the drop on, then disarmed and knocked out. The next one met the butt end of Hollis's shotgun and took a nap.

Ahead of them was an entryway to a foyer. On the other side were two tall oak doors. Within, they could only assume, was the man they'd come to see.

Clearly the foyer was a trap, but they gave each other a shrug and went in any way.

The giant Toro stepped out first and grabbed the end of Hollis's shotgun. He pushed the barrel toward the ground before Hollis had a chance to squeeze the trigger.

Barton raised his gun, but Ox stepped around the corner and slapped it away. The two fell into their own scuffle.

A number of armed thugs moved out of hiding then, but if the others had been nervous about shooting their allies before, these guys certainly weren't going to risk shooting at Toro or Ox.

Toro was exceptionally stronger than Hollis, but he held onto his gun anyway. He didn't want to go fisticuffs with the big man if he could help it. If he could get the barrel pointed in the right direction the fight would be over.

Toro yanked on the gun and jerked Hollis around like a rag doll. He lost his grip and fell to the side, right into another of the thugs. Toro reversed the shotgun and brought the butt up to his shoulder. Hollis grabbed the man he'd crashed into and shoved him in front of the shotgun as Toro pulled the trigger.

The upper half of the thug exploded in a red mist. Toro might have had time to work the pump and fire again, but the crimson spray hit his face and staggered him. As he attempted to wipe the blood from his eyes Hollis charged in and punched him in the nose, shattering the cartilage.

A broken nose didn't seem to faze the big man, who backhanded Hollis off his feet.

Toro leveled the shotgun on Hollis again, but the P.I. was quick enough to kick the barrel to the side as the gun roared. A hole appeared on the floor beside him, but Hollis was already kicking his other leg forward into the big man's crotch.

Finally, Hollis thought, as Toro hunched over from the blow. He was starting to think the big bastard was invulnerable.

As Hollis rolled to his feet he risked a glance to assess the situation. Besides Toro and Ox there were three additional thugs. One was helping Toro to his feet. Another was trying to help Ox subdue Barton. A third stood to the side and was trying to line up a shot on Barton.

Hollis tackled him from behind and drove the would-be shooter to the ground. From the corner of his eye he saw Toro rise and pump the shotgun. Hollis threw one solid punch into the face of the thug he'd tackled and then pulled the man on top of him as Toro fired.

If Toro had been wielding a rifle, the round might have gone through the man and into Hollis. As it was, the buckshot sunk into the thug on top of him, killing the man, but not exiting his body.

Toro worked the pump and fired again. If he'd taken a moment to aim he might have hit Hollis, but he was too full of rage for intelligent thought.

Hollis scooped up the dead thug's firearm and popped off several shots in rapid succession. He didn't bother taking the time to aim, just fired in Toro's general direction. Toro dove for cover while the goon beside him took a round in the leg.

On the other side of the room, Barton struggled with a man trying to subdue him from behind. Ox drew his gun and pointed the barrel at Barton's face. By the time Hollis aimed his own gun, Ox fired.

For a moment Hollis thought Barton was dead, but the bounty hunter had dropped his hip at the last possible moment. The bullet went over the top of his head and struck the thug behind him.

Apparently Ox thought he was dead too and Barton tagged him with a sucker punch, slapped his gun away, and drove another fist into his face.

Hollis turned back to focus on his own problem, which was running across the room toward him while simultaneously pointing a shotgun in his direction. Pinned beneath the dead man still, he was a sitting duck. Hollis pushed the corpse clear and rolled to the side as the gun went off. He rolled again as Toro pumped the shotgun. Toro tried to lead him, but Hollis cut back and rolled the direction he'd come as the gun roared again.

Hollis tried to raise his own gun, but the big man closed the distance between them and kicked it out of his hand. Toro planted a foot on Hollis's chest and stuck the gun barrel in his face. He pulled the trigger again but this time there was only a dull click. The gun was empty.

Undeterred, Toro flipped the shotgun up and attempted to slam the butt down on Hollis's head. The P.I. dodged sideways and the gun smacked against the hardwood.

Hollis grabbed a hold of the shotgun while simultaneously kicking out at Toro's knee. Toro dropped his full weight down on Hollis and turned the gun sideways to try to choke him. Hollis took a two-armed grip but knew he couldn't hold up against Toro's strength. He had a better idea. He let his grip off the butt side, put both hands on the pump, and pushed with everything he had. Like a teeter-totter, the butt came down and smacked him in the face while the barrel popped up and hit Toro in the face. Neither blow impacted enough to hurt, but Toro screamed as the hot metal seared the flesh of his cheek.

He attempted to pull away and Hollis pushed harder to keep the burning metal against his face.

Barton and Ox's fight spilled into theirs when Ox threw Barton right into Toro, knocking him off of Hollis.

"Hey," Barton said as he landed on Hollis. He was rather cheerful despite two swelling eyes, a broken nose, and a stream of blood on his face. "These guys are tough."

"You're telling me," Hollis replied.

"Want to trade?"

"Sure," Hollis replied. "Let's finish this."

They rolled away and set eyes on their targets.

Toro started to rise, but was so consumed with rage at Hollis that Barton caught him off guard with a vicious eye poke. Toro screamed and jerked away, which gave Barton an open shot at his throat. The bounty hunter pelted him in the Adam's apple and then kicked him in the ribs.

At the same time, Ox charged Barton. He, too, was so consumed with rage that he didn't notice Hollis, who snatched up the shotgun and swung it like a baseball bat right into the running man's face. He hit the ground like a brick.

Around them their enemies lay beaten or dead. Neither spoke as they each dug around the mess in search of loaded guns. When they each had one, they headed for the office.

Together they kicked open the door and strolled inside.

King sat alone behind a large oak desk, the golden 1911 in his hands. Hollis and Barton both trained their weapons on him, but instead of trying to shoot them he raised the gun to his own head.

Before he could pull the trigger, Hollis's gun went off. The round struck King just above the elbow. He screamed and the gun fell to the floor.

"My arm!" he screamed. "You bastard!"

"Yeah, I'm the dickhead here."

Both men kept their guns on King and moved closer.

"It's over," Hollis said. "We've got you."

He nodded. "Yes, I surrender."

"Damn right you do," Barton said. "And I have a mind to put a few more rounds in you just for good measure."

Despite his obvious pain, he said, "I admit, you both performed beyond my expectation."

Hollis asked, "Why did you drag us into all of this?"

He shrugged. "Doesn't matter, does it? Call your cop friend, Hollis. You have me dead to rights."

Hollis stared at him for a few moments. In their previous conversations this man had always been so sure and confident, but here he was, done. He'd ensnared them in a spider's web and outsmarted them every step of the way, but now that they were here, he was just giving up? Hollis thought through everything that had happened, his mind racing. Then it clicked.

"Son of a bitch," Hollis said. "You're not King, you're not the Ghost."

"What are you talking about? You got me. You won. It's over."

"No," Hollis said. "You aren't him, are you?"

"What the hell is going on?" Barton asked.

"He's a fake," Hollis said. "That trophy Clutch bashed the thug with. I recognized it. It was an acting award, wasn't it?"

King didn't respond.

"I don't know what's going on," Barton said. "But this is definitely the guy we saw shoot James."

"Yeah," Hollis said. "But you aren't the one pulling the strings, are you?"

King remained silent.

"Then who is?" Barton asked, then almost immediately added, "Shit, where's our pal Terrell?"

"He's not here," Hollis said. "It's him, isn't it? He's the one running the show. You're just some washed up actor doing his dirty work."

The man cringed from pain, but said, "I never had much choice in the matter. I fell in debt with some bad people and I couldn't get work. Once King gets his claws into you, you have to do what he says. There's no way around it. I never wanted to kill anyone."

"And you're supposed to take the fall," Hollis said. "That's why you tried to kill yourself."

He nodded. "King said if my men could kill you, then I was home free. He'd give me a million dollars and I was out. *But*, if you two got to me then I had to continue being him and take the fall."

"I still don't get it," Barton said. "Why set us up?"

"I honestly don't know," the man said. "Please, can you get me help before I bleed to death?"

"After what you did to James, you can sit there and bleed,"

49

Hollis said. "Speaking of which, why him? Why kill a mentally handicapped man?"

The imposter laughed. "James wasn't always like that. From what I understand, he was a brilliant accountant."

"What happened to him?" Barton asked.

"He tried to get out." The imposter shrugged. "He tried to leave King's service. They did that to him. Fed him enough experimental drugs to fry his brain. King kept him around as an example, but I guess the joke was on him, James had enough capacity to escape, at least for a short time."

"And you killed him," Hollis said. "Shot him point blank in the head."

"It's not like I had a choice." He looked down at his destroyed elbow and went a shade paler. "I'm going to bleed out."

"Wouldn't that be a shame," Barton said.

"Where's King now?" Hollis asked.

"Gone," he said. "I think you impressed him. I don't think he expected you to move that fast. He disappeared a few hours ago."

"One last question," Hollis said. "How can we find him?"

The actor laughed. "You can't find him. He's a ghost."

Then he passed out.

***

"Here's to being alive," Hollis said as he raised his shot glass.

Barton, Irma Deuce, and Clutch did the same. They were back at the Hideaway and there was something of a bustling crowd.

After their drinks were down Clutch said, "Damn, you two look like shit."

"It's not so bad," Barton said with a grin. He looked like he'd taken more of a beating, but Hollis felt the way Barton's face looked. It had been a tough fight.

"So what now?" Deuce asked.

Hollis sighed. "I don't know."

"You're just going to let this Ghost, or King, or whoever the hell he is, get away with this?"

Hollis and Barton looked at one another, then both shrugged. Hollis said, "We don't have any leads. He disappeared without a trace. What else can we do? Andrew Goldsmith was the imposter and the one who shot James. He's at the hospital now, but he's going to jail as soon as he's stable. He's so scared of King I imagine he'll say he killed James just like he's supposed to. He's going to prison for murder. But King... He's gone."

Deuce turned to Barton. "So what about you, country boy? You staying in Angeltown?"

"Hell no," he said. "I hate this damn place. I need to see some trees. Find some normal people who don't want to kill me."

"Heading home, then?" Hollis asked.

"First thing in the morning," Barton replied. "I'm ready to put Los Angeles in my rearview mirror."

"Hell, if we had any sense we'd probably go with you," Hollis said.

"Nah," Barton replied. "This is who you are, Hollis. You and I are much the same and we do what we do. The only difference is where we do it. I belong in the mountains made by God. You belong in the mountains made by men."

"Damn, Barton," Deuce said. "That was deep. I didn't know you had it in you."

"I'm full of surprises, gorgeous."

"And immediately back to being an ass," she said.

He smiled again. "But hey, y'all should load up and come visit sometime. It'd do you good."

Hollis chuckled. "So instead of getting shot at in a concrete jungle I can get shot at in a real jungle?"

"Forest," Barton said. "You'd be getting shot at in a forest."

"What's the difference?"

"How the hell should I know?"

"I'm going to miss you, country boy."

"Yeah, you too, big city."

***

The next morning Hollis woke up to his phone ringing. He groaned as he rolled over to grab it. His whole body hurt like hell, but that was all forgotten when he saw that the number was unknown.

He answered.

"Hello, Hollis," the voice of the supposed Terrell Davis said.

51

"How are you feeling this morning?"

"What do you want?"

"I wanted to thank you," he said. "You did excellent."

"What was the point of all of this?"

"Well, partially for business."

"You set us up to take down your competitors."

"Exactly."

"You're planning on taking over the drug and sex trade in L.A.?"

"I wouldn't say taking it over. I've had a rather large stake in it for some time. But it's important to keep profit margins up."

"So that's it? You just used us to get to your competitors?"

"Somewhat, yes. I also did it for my own personal amusement. I don't like Los Angeles. It's a boring cesspit. You offered some measure of entertainment while I concluded my work here. *And* I was testing you. Both of you. I wanted to know if you're as good as you're rumored to be. I assure you I wasn't disappointed."

"Yeah, it sounds like we did real good. It sounds like we almost had you."

"Mr. Goldsmith talks too much. It's the curse of self-important actors. Sure, it probably would have been more beneficial for you to simply die. And I must admit, I found it a bit irritating that you solved this as quickly as you did. There may have to be some retribution for that, Nathaniel." He sighed. "But again, I was testing you, and you passed."

"And why would you care about that?"

"Because I may have work for you at some point."

"I'll never work for you."

"Of course you will. If I so choose, then you will. You did this time, didn't you?"

"Yeah, but now I know your game. You won't trick me again."

He chuckled. "Sure I will. And even if I don't, there are other motivators besides money."

"Such as?"

"Oh, I don't know," he said. "Perhaps a man in my position might have information about dear old dad's murder."

Hollis remained silent.

"See," he said. "Pulling the strings is what I do."

"I won't work for you," Hollis repeated. "And if you come to Angeltown again, I will find you."

"We'll see. When I do return to Angeltown, you may want to ensure that I don't find you first."

"I can't figure out if you're threatening me or trying to hire me."

"Could be both. We'll find out I suppose. Something tells me we'll meet again. In the meantime, do take care of yourself, Nathaniel. I'd hate for something to happen to you before we get a chance to reunite."

"Yeah, you go straight to hell."

His laughter echoed in the P.I.'s head long after the call ended.

KING COW

by
Gary Phillips

Nate Hollis was let into the suite by an aging, attractive woman in a business skirt and print blouse, the sleeves at half-mast. "Mr. Hollis. I appreciate you coming at such short notice. Does that speak to the hold Monica has on you?"

He smiled. "Something like that, Ms. DeHavilland."

Hollis removed his hat, which she took and sat properly upside down on its crown on a side table. The fragrance of fresh flowers permeated the rooms, though there seemed to be none evident.

"Have a seat," she said, indicating a small table and chairs near a window. On the table were two covered plates and two silver coffee pots sent up from room service. Morning light glowed in the room.

"Coffee?" she asked.

"Yes, thank you."

She poured him some and removed the food covers. He was pleasantly surprised to see crisp bacon, sausage patties, eggs over easy, and wheat toast.

"I sure you don't eat like this normally, Ms. DeHavilland."

"Am I so old and decrepit that you can't call me Kara?" She displayed snowy teeth in a relatively unlined face. "Imagine being vain at my age."

Monica Orozco, his lawyer friend, had set this meeting up. She'd told Hollis that DeHavilland looked sixty but was near to eighty. Orozco had been mistaken. DeHavilland didn't look fifty-five to him.

"What can I do for you, Kara?"

"What all did Monica tell you, Nate? And please, eat, won't you?" She handed him a spade-shaped spatula. She poured hot water from one of the small pots into her cup to steep her teabag.

Hollis said as he served himself, "Not a whole lot. She called me before daybreak today and told me you, well, your company, is a client and you two also sit on a board of a literacy organization. She said you were in town as Earth Harvest is putting on some sort of conference in a few days, and there's a concern about your main keynote speaker who has gone missing."

He started eating then added, "But as usual, she played it close to the vest and said you'd fill me in." Orozco had called on his cell while he was sleeping in the bed of Tyra Williams, owner of indie record label Go-Goh records. Williams wasn't happy about being awakened at that hour, especially by an ex-girlfriend of Hollis', and she pointedly let him know that.

Kara DeHavilland took in and let out a breath. "What do you know about the term 'food insecurity?'"

He made a small gesture as he chewed and swallowed. "Essentially not being able to provide enough food for yourself or your family." He had more of his breakfast, a stab of guilt coming and going.

"That, in a nutshell, is what the conference is about." She dipped her teabag in and out of the hot water. "Just to get on my soapbox for a moment, suffice it to say that in the U.S. alone, nearly fifty million people are food insecure on any given day. Let alone people in Haiti after their devastating quake, the Sudanese because of the ongoing conflict in their country, parts of the former Soviet Union, and so many other areas of our world. There are many reasons for this, but it isn't because we don't have the wherewithal to feed everybody."

"Were it so simple," he echoed.

"Indeed, for all sorts of geo-political reasons, internal corruption issues and other factors, these prevent people from not being able to get enough food, or too often food that is filling but not nutritious."

Hollis eschewed forking in more food and said, "This gets us back to the keynoter?"

"The speaker is Jethro Emmanuel. And he's gone missing since two or so this morning."

Hollis said, "Dr. Jet Emanuel? The former assistant secretary of agriculture under President Clinton?"

"You're not old enough to remember that."

Now he smiled. "You'd be surprised. What's he been up to lately? Oh, of course," he added, "that's the subject of his talk isn't it?"

"Yes," she said. "A presentation some would not like him to make."

"What was he working on?" He had more of his breakfast.

"You're eating it."

"Huh?"

"In vitro meat."

Hollis regarded the piece of sausage he'd just speared on the tines of his fork. "This was grown in a Petri dish?" He ate it, this time trying to discern if the taste was different than other sausage he'd eaten. "This is pretty good," he admitted. He had more bacon too.

"This has been going on for some time," DeHavilland said. "Trying to replicate meat, beef and pork mainly, in laboratories. Fish is a much fussier process. Anyway, scientists have been taking stem cells from live animals or even freshly slaughtered ones. The cells are immersed in a kind of soup of glucose, amino acids and minerals, proteins."

"The cells grow?" Hollis asked.

She sipped her tea, nodding. "The usual result is a fibrous, gelatinous mass that does not look appetizing, has no marbling, and frankly has less protein. While it is free of the antibiotics and chances of E. coli infection, our mass produced cultured meat is not something I'd put on the shelves of my stores."

"But Dr. Emmanuel has advanced the process." Hollis dabbed at his mouth with a cloth napkin.

She looked off then. "Very much so. To the point the ABA is worried." A bemused look shaped her features.

Confused, Hollis said, "Why would a defunct pro basketball league be out to get him?"

Now she looked lost for a moment. "Oh. I meant the American Beef Association."

"Big cattle types whose economic interests don't coincide with meat you can grow like carrots."

57

"Yes. But Dr. Emmanuel's process could be a breakthrough regarding hunger issues." She reached across and had a piece of his bacon. Hollis figured that was her caloric count for the day.

He asked, "Could they have snatched him?"

She sat back, crossing her legs. "I like the way your mind works, Nate. That was the first thought that came to me and I checked. They haven't."

"You checked? You have a spy in the ABA?"

"I keep a close watch."

"He disappeared from here? I mean, in town?" They were in her suite at the Four Seasons Hotel in Beverly Hills.

"We had Dr. Emmanuel set up in a disguised lab so he could prepare some product for display and the eating enjoyment of those attending the conference. It's in the part of town called Pico Union near downtown Los Angeles. Are you familiar with that area?"

"I am." When Hollis had been an investigator for the D.A.'s office, he'd been on a case once and was ambushed outside a dance hall down there. He didn't mention this. "I assume you've secured his lab?"

"Awaiting your trained eyes," she said. "My gal Friday Justine will meet you there."

They discussed several other particulars, including his fee, and he left with a flash drive containing information about Emmanuel's work. Outside, after handing the valet his parking ticket, two tall men approached him. One wore sunglasses, the other a stylish Stetson.

The one in the sunglasses said, "Mr. Hollis, my name is McAlester. How would you like to make half a million dollars? Tax free?"

Hollis grinned. "Make it a million."

McAlester didn't hesitate. "A million it is."

"I'm pretty sure that's my price, only I'd have sleepless nights turning over Dr. Emmanuel to you beef boys."

"You can buy a lot of sleep aids for a million," Stetson said.

"I imagine that's so. Too bad I won't find out."

"There're other ways of persuading you," Stetson said. One of his large hands was upraised, and he rubbed those knuckles with the other hand. An ostentatious ring was displayed as well.

"It's been tried."

Stetson cocked his head to one side. McAlester made an open palms gesture. "Have a good day." The two walked off as Hollis' car arrived.

"Sweet ride, man," the valet remarked about Hollis' restored '68 Dodge Dart with the Crager rims.

"Right on." He tipped the valet and drove away, then pulled over several blocks later on a residential street marked for permit parking only. He got out and felt around the underside of his car. Inside the rear left wheel well he found a magnetic tracking device. It was rectangular and not much bigger than a lighter. He stepped on the thing, smashing it, and then wiped his hands off with a rag from his trunk. Thereafter he went south on Beverly Drive as the morning rush hour thinned.

At Olympic Boulevard he turned, a James Hunter CD, *People Gonna Talk,* playing on his car's music system. Driving along, the skyscrapers of a gentrified downtown loomed in the east. Eventually he arrived mid-block on Catalina Street at what was once a carniceria, a Mexican-style neighborhood meat market. The establishment had been boarded up by the health department. There was still a life-sized plastic bull on the flat roof, overlooking the street below. He parked at the curb. On the north side of the building was a driveway leading to the rear.

"Hello, Mr. Hollis." Justine Duluz greeted him, extending her hand. She was a striking blonde with a downhill skier's build. Hollis imagined she maintained her tan playing volleyball at the beach in a string bikini. She wore a dark pantsuit and flat shoes. There was a thumb ring on her right hand, and she was holding an iPhone. Duluz looked past him, brows furrowed concerning his car.

He shook her hand. "Yeah, I know, not exactly doing my part for smaller carbon footprints. But it does run good."

"I'm sure," she said and he followed her through the entrance, a set of double doors. They stood in the shallow and bare front portion of the building, and Duluz punched in a code to a metal door with a reinforced window set in it at eye level. The door slid open and the two stepped into a modern laboratory agleam with chrome and glass.

Hollis looked at various pieces of boneless beef of varying thicknesses and shapes, some with marbling and some without, sitting in clear Pyrex casserole dishes along one long low table. Wires with pronged ends were sunk into the meat leading to active monitors.

"Trippy," he muttered.

"Frankenmeat is alive," she joked.

"This meat looks real." He corrected himself. "I mean, like it was recently carved from a side of beef."

"Yes, the work product is amazing, isn't it? He was even perfecting how to duplicate spare ribs using a kind of molded template as the bones." She added, "Dr. Emmanuel had living quarters above."

"You have a record of his incoming and outgoing phone calls?"

"We're not the Gestapo, Mr. Hollis," she said sweetly.

"Call me Nate." They headed toward some carpeted stairs through an arched doorway. "So no idea if he got a frantic call? Does he have relatives out here? Grown children?" The two ascended the stairs.

She held up her iPhone. "I'm getting what we know together from our headquarters in Portland. Though, understand Dr. Emmanuel was paid as a consultant to Earth Harvest, so there may not be a lot."

"Okay," Hollis said. Entering the Spartanly furnished apartment, Hollis made a call on his cell phone. "Hey, Kristy, it's me. Can you have one of your researchers hit me back? I want to know what you have in your archives on Dr. Jethro Emmanuel...yes, that Jethro Emmanuel. Particularly his childhood and formative years. Email it to me if you can." He asked for and repeated Duluz's email address into his phone.

He paused, aware Duluz could hear him. "I'll work it out in trade, huh?" Hollis ended his message to Kristy Simons, the publisher of the online and hardcopy political and cultural tabloid, *L.A. Voice.*

"You look through his things?"

"Nope. I waited for you. No disturbing the crime scene, right?"

"I hope it's not one." He began searching the premises – a main room, kitchenette, bedroom and bathroom. "How long had he been staying here?" Hollis noted a ball of cotton in the bedroom's wastebasket, like the kind you'd remove from a bottle of pills.

"About two weeks," she said. "Prepping for the conference."

"And you filled a prescription for him?"

"Yes," she noted, impressed. "Heart condition."

He kept poking around. "Did he drink? Like the ponies or strip clubs? Or liked to get all Brokeback with boys with broad shoulders? Not that there's anything wrong with that."

She snorted. "I wasn't his tour guide nor procurer, Mr. Hollis, just his liaison." She crossed her arms, observing him.

Hollis noted the well-toned arms of the liaison. Emmanuel's pants, underwear and T-shirts were folded on a standing metal rack, his pressed shirts hung on wire hangers in a small closet.

"He had two bags; one is gone, a soft-sided piece of luggage," Duluz said, looking at the shelf in the closet.

"He packed light, expecting to come back?" Hollis mused. "Or had to leave in a hurry and took what he could heft. He had a car?"

"Yes, we'd gotten him a rental, a late model Camry. I know he used it this past weekend but right now it's parked out back."

"Rental agencies put GPS devices in their cars. Can you see if they'd tell you where it went?"

"I'm sure they'd shine me on, but maybe Kara has some pull. I'll call her."

"Good," Hollis said. "So did someone come by to get him or did he call a cab?"

She hunched a shoulder and made the call.

He continued looking around. In the refrigerator were several items, including a bag from a fast food place called Gus's with a logo on it. He looked in the bag and saw a container of a partially eaten taco salad.

"I saw a laptop downstairs in the lab. Did the doc use that for his notes?" He asked over his shoulder, looking back at Duluz.

"We provided one to him but he also had his own. Not sure which is downstairs but I'm betting it's ours."

It was, and there was no indication on the computer where Emmanuel might have gone.

"Okay," Duluz said, after thumbing off her iPhone. I called Yellow Cab and Bell Cab; neither of them have a record of picking up a fare from this address early this morning."

"Let's take a trip to Gus's," Hollis said, getting up from perusing one of the files on the flash drive DeHavilland had given him. There was also a printer, and he'd printed out several copies of Emmanuel's photo.

"Why, you hungry?"

"It's all about the field work, Ms. Duluz. Anyway, it's better than sitting around waiting for your boss to call back." He folded the printouts in half and put them inside his sport coat pocket. They began walking to the fast food place. Hollis knew where Gus's was because he'd been there several times in the past. It wasn't too far away. They passed graffitied walls and empty storefronts.

At a light pole, Hollis regarded a handbill taped on it advertising Matanzas Cab Enterprises. The flyer was in Spanish, which wasn't unusual given that the Pico Union section was heavily Latino. The company's phone number was repeated vertically across the bottom. Scissors had been used to snip between each number so passersby could pull the digits off for future reference. Hollis picked off a slip and handed it across to Duluz.

"Yellow and Bell service downtown but probably won't come this way at that time of the morning. Not enough expensive fares in a low-income area, don't you know. This outfit is local. Cómo está tu español?"

"Lo suficientemente bueno," she said.

A low rider '65 Impala, loaded with four men, drove by heading in the opposite direction on the street. The driver, who had a bandana tied around his head, whistled at Duluz as they passed. She all but rolled her eyes.

Hollis suddenly stopped, gripping Duluz's upper arm as she was dialing the cab company's number.

"Hey," she remarked, pulling her arm free.

"I bet you jog."

"Yeah, why?"

"Because I'm an idiot. I found the tracer they wanted me to find. We've got to get back to the lab. Now." He started running back the way they'd come.

"Are you high, Hollis?" She made an exasperated sound and took off too.

They got back to Catalina and the lowered Impala was parked behind Hollis' Dart. The double doors were open. They crouched down at the corner where there was some shrubbery.

"How did you—?" Duluz began.

"Is there another way into the lab?"

"Yes, there's a metal back door to the apartment. Stairs in back. I have a key."

"Good. I'm going to keep them busy while you go in and get the goods."

She nodded curtly. "All right."

"Hold on." Hollis ran again, this time into a discount store several doors down on Pico Boulevard. He returned shortly with a can of turpentine. There was some newspaper blown against a nearby cyclone fence and he rolled this up as a wick in the can after unscrewing the top.

"Get ready," he said and ran over to the Impala. There were shouts from inside and Hollis threw his lit can on the back of the car. The turpentine spread, aflame over the rear of the car.

"Motherfucker," one of the men said, running out. He swung a pry bar but Hollis ducked and threw his body sideways into the man's torso, bowling him over. He'd gotten a quick look inside, and could see the men were using this and another pry bar to get the inner sliding metal door open. Hollis slugged the man he was grappling with twice but was hauled to his feet by other hands on him. Stetson grinned broadly.

"You're an ornery cuss, ain't you?"

"Some people are taken with my charm."

"That right?" Stetson smiled and punched him hard in the gut. Hollis sagged. "Hold the Bronze Buckaroo up," the puncher said to the two latched onto the private eye. They did.

"Where's Emmanuel?"

"Bonin' your mama," Hollis cracked.

That earned him a sock on the jaw, blood spraying. "You got some mouth on you."

Hollis reared back and bringing his knees up, drove his heels into Stetson's chest. This sent him backward and loosened the grip of one of the men holding him. Hollis got a fist free and hit the other man. He dropped to the ground and grabbed the pry bar. He came up swinging, connecting with the rib cage of one of his attackers.

"Back the fuck off," Hollis warned. The men circled around him. Stetson lunged and Hollis hit him with the bar across his face, knocking him to the ground.

"How you like me now?" Hollis jibbed as Stetson swore a string of profanities.

Justine Duluz's Prius came fast out of the driveway of the carniceria, the passenger door wide open.

"Let's bounce, slugger," she advised.

Hollis waved the pry bar back and forth, keeping the others from rushing him. He jumped in the car and they drove away.

"This here dance ain't done yet, hombre," Stetson yelled, a hand to the side of his wounded face. The four rushed to the Impala, the flames having gone out as the turpentine was consumed.

"Punch it, Ms. Duluz," Hollis said. "Let's see what this wheat grass burner can do."

"We've got a head start, but no way we can outrun a V8," she said.

"You're right. Head to the Convention Center."

She flicked a look at him. "Okay."

On the back seat was a cardboard box containing the lab grown meat. The laptop was on the seat too. As they tore down Pico, they could see the Impala in the rearview. She shot through a red light, nearly colliding with a bobtail delivery truck. Brakes screeched, horns honked and drivers swore. Their pursuers got snarled at the light, giving them a few moments.

"I like your style," Hollis remarked.

She winked at him, laughing nervously. They got to the nearby Convention Center on Figueroa, stretching between Pico and Venice Boulevards. Directly to the north was the Staples Center where the pro basketball teams the Comets and Lakers played. Next to that was the L.A. Live complex that included a hotel and night clubs. Hollis told her to drive into the parking structure.

"We'll be trapped."

"That's where we'll lose them," he promised.

They entered. There was a boat show at the Center so there were cars in the elevated structure. As they went up a ramp, the two spotted the Impala lining up behind other cars to enter the lot.

"Take this level," Hollis said.

The Prius went along and they parked between two SUVs. Stepping out, Hollis carried the cardboard box, Duluz the laptop.

They trotted and went through a door and down a set of exit stairs.

"This way," Hollis pointed as they got to the second level.

They hurried and after more directing from Hollis, soon were in a service hallway that emptied inside the Staples Center.

"How'd you know to get us here?' Duluz asked.

Hollis grinned and said, "There's a car rental place on Venice and Grand, a few blocks away. " He started walking toward the exit. She caught up.

"And how'd you know the beef association's crew was in that lowrider?"

"The one in the cowboy hat was with a man named McAlester outside of Kara's hotel. He wears a big, fancy ring. When the Impala rolled past, I saw the hand of someone sitting in the back seat on the open window frame of the car.

"You saw the ring on his finger."

"Right."

"So how do we find Dr. Emmanuel?"

"I'm working on that."

***

By the time they got out to Chino in San Bernardino County, Hollis had learned Earth Harvest – an upscale grocery chain specializing in quality foods such as grain fed as opposed to corn fed beef—planned to convert the carniceria into one of its markets through its foundation that sponsored the likes of inner city nutrition programs. Also that Justine Duluz was a graduate in cultural anthropology and had worked for Kara DeHavilland going on four years.

It was past noon and the temperature had climbed into the high eighties. Kristy Simons had emailed several pertinent articles about Jet Emmanuel, who'd grown up in the Southern California's Whittier. One piece on him, from *Esquire* back when he was in the Clinton administration, mentioned that when he was a child, his folks would take him and his sister out to the working ranch a grandmother had here in Chino.

The rental outfit had been obstinate about releasing information on where Emmanuel had taken the car over the weekend, but from the cab company they'd learned Dr. Emmanuel had been taken to

Union Station, where the trains came and went. Backtracking the schedules, Hollis zeroed in on an Amtrak run that went through Chino. They parked the rental at the city hall complex on Central. Thereafter Hollis and Duluz found the assessor's office. Because they had the full name of the grandmother from the *Esquire* article, Hollis was able to locate the title report and other data, including the address, concerning the family ranch.

"So you really think we're going to find him out here?" Duluz asked as Hollis drove. She consulted the map on the navigation monitor. "Why all of a sudden would he come back here?"

"If we find him, we can ask him, my good woman. If not, then we keep looking."

She smiled at him.

Their route took them past a ramshackle arena they could see into through openings of wooden bleachers lined in sheet and corrugated metal ringing them around the inside.

"What the hell's that?' Duluz said.

"Demolition derby track I think," Hollis answered.

"You a fan, huh?"

"Drive those beaters around held together with bailing wire and prayer, bashing into each other. Big fun."

She chuckled. Duluz had taken off her coat. She wore a short sleeved thin blouse. A Maori-style tattoo encircled a muscular arm. Hollis refocused. They got turned around but eventually found the ranch. The smell and sound of livestock was prevalent. Hollis parked the rental and the two walked up to the front door under a covered porch. Hollis knocked as Duluz peered inside through a curtained window.

"See anything?" he asked.

"No."

"And no answer." He rattled the doorknob. "We could break in."

"That's probably not wise."

"Shit," Hollis swore, turning to look out onto the dirt lane they'd come down.

"Now what, Rockford?"

He started around back, Duluz following him.

"You hate being wrong, don't you?"

He glared back at her and she snickered. There was a gate and fence of wood with heavy wire that led to the rear of the house, which looked out over a pasture area. Several cows grazed and wandered about. A padlock secured the gate. Hollis clambered over the fence, as did Duluz. He bent slightly and put his face to a window in the back door, looking in on a kitchen out of a Norman Rockwell painting including an old-fashioned stove.

"I think he's been here," Hollis said. He moved aside to allow her a look.

On a kitchen table replete with a red and white checkered table cloth sat an open laptop, sheets of paper, and a plate with remnants of food. "Yeah, that looks like his computer," Duluz agreed. She straightened. "But where is he now?"

Hollis was standing on the grass, pointing further into the pasture. "Isn't that him?"

Duluz stared at some cows milling about a man with his hands down at his side. "Doctor Emmanuel," she yelled, coming off the steps and running toward the figure some 200 yards away. "Doctor Emmanuel," she repeated.

Heading toward him, suddenly more cows were between them and their quarry. Hollis looked to his right and could see part of a barbed wire fence had been taken down. The animals were coming from that direction. The cows weren't charging but seemed to intentionally put their bulk in the way, as if herding the two.

"Dammit," Duluz said as a cow streamed its body waste at her feet.

"This is amazing," Hollis said. "Cows on their own don't operate in a pattern. But these lil doggies are in lock step like a troop movement. And they're not making a sound." The bespectacled Emmanuel was facing them, grinning like a demented seraphim. There was now at least the length of two train cars of cows between them and the biologist. The cows were hemming the two in tight, but in an orderly fashion.

"Dr. Doolittle is controlling them. I guess his research has unlocked beef mind power." Hollis held up his hands in mock horror.

"Idiot," Duluz snorted. She looked over to Emmanuel, who was smiling. "That's crazy, Hollis."

"Let us go," Hollis yelled to the older man standing at the periphery of the herd. "We just want to help you, doc."

The man gave a half wave, turned, and walked away. Hollis and Duluz tried to get through, but the harder they pushed, the more the cows pushed back. The detective put an arm around her waist as a cow rammed her.

"Shit," she blurted. "What the hell, huh?"

Hollis watched Jethro Emmanuel's form get smaller as he walked to another farmhouse and barn and disappeared among the buildings. Minutes later the cows broke formation and returned to normal – mooing and chewing grass, moving about aimlessly.

Duluz looked at Hollis. "Ideas?"

"Find out why he was here."

"Where do we start?"

"Break into the damn house first," he announced, walking toward his goal. There was a small window on a bathroom off the back porch cracked open for air. Though he was too big to squeeze through, Justine Duluz managed with ease when he boosted her up.

"I'm impressed," Hollis said as she went through, his eyes on her shapely backside.

"About my ass or my burglary skills, Nate?"

"Both," he admitted. She let him in through the back door. As she attempted to discern Emmanuel's password on his laptop, Hollis prowled about. Presently he returned to the kitchen.

"Any luck?" he asked.

"Not yet," she said.

He jerked a head toward a wall. "There are some Anzemet pills along with other medications in the bedroom." He paused then continued, "It's to combat nausea when you're getting chemotherapy treatments."

"Emmanuel?"

"His sister it seems," Hollis said.

"She died early this morning in the hospital. They must have called him and he came out here." McAlester said, standing in the suddenly open back doorway to the ranch house. Stetson was with him, the side of his face swollen. He glared at Hollis. McAlester held a gun. Both came further into the room. Duluz stood.

"Been doing your homework," Hollis commented.

"We got nothing but resources, old sport." McAlester gestured with the gun at Stetson. "Fetch the computer and we can bid these two adieu."

"Another time," Stetson said to Hollis, coming closer to the kitchen table.

"Whatever excuse works for you, Sally." He made a kissy sound. "It's not like you're man enough to take me without that gat here."

"No, he's—" McAlester began but it was too late. Stetson took the bait and charged Hollis.

The private eye had gone low and wrapped his arms around the other man's waist, trying to shove him into McAlester. But he knew what Hollis was trying to do and simply clubbed Stetson with his gun to get him out of the way. Duluz had acted simultaneously. She grabbed the laptop and threw it in the sink, turning on the faucets. She got out of the way as McAlester ran over, waving the piece.

"Move, get out the way," he barked. He took the wet laptop in one hand, tucking it under an arm. "Let's go," he told a dazed Stetson. They left.

"Wow," Duluz said, breathing hard.

"Guess we better call your boss."

After that they got something to eat – salads for both of them— they went to the demolition derby that evening.

"I bet Number Five, the Plymouth, to finish." Duluz said as they sat in the stands. She smiled and scooted closer to Hollis, putting a hand on his leg.

He put an arm around her shoulders. "I like my boy in the Camaro." Out on the track amid the mechanized frenzy, a green Gremlin with the roof partially caved in T-boned an LTD. The crowd yelled their approval.

"You're on," she said. They shook on it.

Later, in their room in the 1930s era Hughes Hotel off the highway, Hollis sat on the couch as Justine Duluz slowly came toward him. At one point earlier that day in Chino, after their lunch, she'd gone into a Goodwill Store near where they'd eaten. When she was shopping, he'd been checking out some vintage vehicles on a used car lot. Hollis didn't know then what she'd bought given the items were in a paper bag. Now he knew.

The short cotton dress she wore had a faint pattern on it. The dragonfly tattoo on her calve was prominent against her tanned skin. Duluz straddled his lap, pressing the hunting knife flat against his cheek. She was into role play. He breathed heavily.

"Eva of the SS will have her way with you, my downed bronze American flyer." She said in a kind *Hogan's Heroes* kind of German accent. She tossed the rubber knife on the couch and did indeed have her way with him. A bet was a bet and he'd lost. Still, she must have planned this kinky fantasy since the afternoon— must be something about danger and cattle he reflected, as lust overtook his senses and body.

***

Kara DeHavilland's spy in the American Beef Association informed her that no data was recovered from Jethro Emanuel's laptop. Though there were some notes about his process, so far other scientists Earth Harvest employed couldn't duplicate his results with taste and texture of Emmanuel's in vitro meat.

A month or so later, Hollis was watching CNN. Captured on the shaky video of a cell phone, was an indistinct figure standing on the edge of a massive feedlot outside Broken Bow, Nebraska. This figure raised his arms from the side of his body, palms up, and suddenly the cattle, in an orderly and disciplined fashion, trampled down their side gates and thousands of heads of cattle followed this figure. This caused a massive disruption and property damage in town as the cattle marched through, unheeding wranglers who sought to round them up.

Thereafter the ABA put out a million dollar bounty on Dr. Jethro Emanuel.

A TRIP TO SCHOOL

By
Scott Adlerberg

"It's gonna get ugly, Nate."

"This is a public school?"

"Charter."

"For what grades?" Nate asked.

"Kindergarten through fifth."

"Morris, damn, you're talking about children."

"It's the parents," Morris said. "The kids are fine."

"What about the parents?"

"Not just them really. It's the principal, the board. The adults overall, you could say."

Nate wondered how a school could be so messy that his old friend, a guy he hadn't seen in nearly ten years, would want him to fly across the country to see it. He'd be getting involved in…what exactly? And to provide what? Protection for his friend? He remembered Morris being in shape and able to handle himself, so if he wanted Nate to have his back for whatever the hell was going on, it had to be damn serious.

"And you're sure this isn't something for the police?"

"Nothing's happened yet, Nate. Nothing drastic."

"Then what?"

"Not enough to call the NYPD. I can't tell them to come prowl around the school waiting for violence to break out."

"Have you tried?"

"It's too complicated. The cops'll think I'm someone with a vendetta, half nuts."

"You were always a little nuts."

"Only in the blackjack days, Nate. Only when I was counting

cards."

"Ever go down there anymore?"

"Nah. No time. Weekdays are for work, weekends the kid."

Well, Nate thought, he didn't have a lot going on now anyway. And a job was a job, cash in hand. Fall in Los Angeles had brought more of the chronic drought, and here he had a chance for something new. November in New York. All that time he'd spent years ago in Atlantic City, why hadn't he ever driven up the Turnpike and visited? He hadn't, for whatever reason, but here, out of nowhere, was his opportunity to go.

"All right," he said. "I can't promise anything."

"I didn't ask you to."

"I gotta scout around to see what you're talking about."

"Thanks, Nate. I'll make the reservations and email you the ticket."

***

Morris picked Nate up at La Guardia Airport, driving a gray rental car.

"Don't you have your own wheels?"

"What for? When I need to drive, I rent."

"New York."

"You'll have to get used to walking again, Nate."

In ten years, Morris had barely aged. He still had a clean-shaven face with smooth skin and the complexion of a lightly roasted coffee ground. His hair, though cut shorter than before, remained black and frizzy. No receding hairline, no paunch. Nothing under his clothes – black pants, a red sweater, and a windbreaker jacket—that didn't look solid. He'd told Nate that he worked out at a gym three times a week, lifting weights, doing the bike machine, so Nate found it hard to believe that he'd be frightened for himself. Had a crazy person at the school, a parent or administrator, threatened him with a weapon? Or was it something worse than that? Someone Morris had a difference with had said he'd hurt Morris' son. No, Morris would have called the police for that.

"You look good, Nate. You're keepin' fit."

"You wouldn't have called me if you thought I wasn't."

They were on the crowded Grand Central Parkway, weaving among the three lanes, and Nate would have liked to banter with Morris. Recollect the shit they'd done way back and fill each other in on what they'd been doing, professions aside, but he wanted clarification about the business causing the anxiety.

"Wanna tell me what I'm doing here, Mo? I mean, I'm glad to see you and all, and appreciate the hospitality – finally a chance to see New York – but let's have it. What am I supposed to be doing for you?"

"You know my son is named Edmund, right?"

"You mentioned it."

"After Edmund Dantes, the Count of Monte Cristo."

Nate couldn't restrain a smile. "That was you, I'll bet, right? Not your wife."

"She got to give the middle name, Francois. After her father."

"And?"

"Since she and I divorced –"

"If this is a custody thing…"

"It isn't, Nate. Jackie and I are cool."

Morris slowed the car down as they approached the Triboro Bridge toll booths, checking the mirror to see whether he could swerve into an E-Z Pass lane.

"I'm hiring you in your official capacity as a PI."

"So long as you know I'm limited here. My license is for California."

Morris looked at him, sober-faced, then back through the windshield.

"First we'll have to talk with Jacqueline. She doesn't know I'm bringing you in, but she shouldn't be a problem."

"What difference does it make if she knows or not?"

"She's stubborn. Not always crazy about accepting help."

"Does she need it?"

"She's been getting threats."

"What kind?"

"Let's talk with her. Also…"

"Yeah?"

"We gotta run my plan by her. No real getting around that."

"You intend to tell me what this plan is?"

The car had stopped in the toll lane, but when the gate swung up, Morris pressed on the gas. They moved forward, into the flow of bridge traffic. Nate was looking across the bridge at the gunmetal sky over Harlem.

"You'll be going undercover in a way, if I can put it like that, pretending to be Edmund's uncle."

***

Jacqueline Perrin, like her ex-husband, was in her late thirties, a striking woman with long dreadlocks and very dark skin. Born in Cameroon but raised in France, as Morris had told Nate, she'd been living in the United States for nine years. She and Morris had met in a bar, "the old fashioned way," Morris said, and they'd married fast, had a kid. Six years later came the divorce. Now she lived on 117th Street near Morningside Park, four blocks from the school Edmund attended, while Morris lived where they had when married, in the Fort Greene section of Brooklyn. They each had a two bedroom apartment, but Edmund stayed with his mother weekdays because of the school's proximity. Edmund was eight, in third grade.

"The threats," Jackie said. "Yes. They've been an issue."

They were in her dining area, just off the kitchen, seated at the table there. Jacqueline had made them all coffee, and Edmund was in his room asleep. She'd made certain he fell asleep before they started talking, reading in his bed to him until his eyes closed. A light in the kitchen was on as well as a lamp in the living room, and through the windows the moon was showing through, full and luminous.

"You know who's doing the threats?" Nate asked.

"It's so fucked up in this school," Morris said. "It could be a few people."

"I can talk for myself," Jackie told him, glowering.

"My bad," Morris said. He smiled at Nate. "Old habits. You want to tell him then?"

So Jackie did, laying it out, the tangle of agendas and rivalries at the school, the power struggles and budget shortfalls. In the three years since its inception, the New York French American Academy had been rife with problems.

"Holy shit," Nate said, when she'd finished. "You're not

exaggerating?"

"Not a word."

"Let me get this straight."

"Ask away."

"You have a faction of parents who liked the old principal –"

"Parents and teachers."

"Right. And they're upset about how she was forced out. It was the Parent Association head who became principal herself."

"Yup."

Nate stared across the table at Morris and Jacqueline, back and forth between them.

"The old principal was French, a white lady but French, and this one's American."

"A white American," Morris said. "Though her mother was French so she can speak the language."

"What's the student body like?"

"Very mixed," Jackie said. "That's the great thing about the school. It's the first school in the city, public or charter, that's specifically a French-English bilingual school. You got parents from France, Morocco, West Africa, Algeria, Switzerland – wherever French is spoken."

"You enrolled your son 'cause you want him to learn French?"

"It's my language," said Jackie.

"And people from Harlem?" Nate asked. "Any kids from here go?"

"Absolutely," Morris said. "If their parents applied. There's a whole bunch of American parents, mostly from Harlem, who don't speak any French who have their kids here."

"Don't sound like your favorites."

"They're not. They're the ones who forced out the old principal."

"The reason being?"

"Too strict, they complained. *Too* French."

"Too French in a French school."

"Hey," said Morris. "I'm repeating what I heard."

"Madame Robbaz pushed hard," Jackie said. "She ran the place like a private school where she came from, and the American parents in particular love to give their input. About everything."

"She wasn't diplomatic enough," Morris said.

"But the new principal is?" Nate asked.

"Heidi," Jackie said, "is a manipulator. No qualifications or experience."

"How the hell did she get the position?"

"Politics," Jackie answered. "The head of the school's board and the people he has in his pocket on it. They put her in for their own reasons."

Nate had drained his coffee cup and was fiddling with his spoon.

"In any case," Jackie continued. "She's a disaster. Now the black American contingent, if you can call them that, can't stand *her*."

"Is she biased?"

"She's condescending. She'll kiss the ass of some parents, the more well-to do, like the white French ones –"

"So they like her?"

"Not all. The French take school seriously and they can see she's not qualified."

"And people whose asses she doesn't kiss?"

"Everyone else. The West Africans. North Africans. Haitians. She treats parents with less means like dirt."

"Pleasant," Nate said.

"I'm pretty sure she's the one behind the threats."

"And you kept what you've gotten?"

"Of course."

"May I?"

Jackie rose to go into the bedroom and get the computer printed notes she'd received, and when she came back and he'd looked them over, Nate asked whether he could take them with him.

"Be my guest."

"I'm eager to meet this principal of yours."

***

As Morris had told him, he found the principal at 9:30 the next morning in a café around the corner from the school. The Patisserie Ambassade was a Senegalese place, and he found her sitting at a table for two with another woman. They made for quite a contrast.

Heidi Zanderlein was a large woman in slacks and a wrinkled blouse, wearing a plain grey sweater with buttons. She had on no makeup and her stringy black hair was arranged in a slightly disheveled ponytail. Her companion, younger, shapely, wore an elegant black business suit and black stockings, and Nate assumed, from her features, that she was African. They were sitting over coffee and croissants when he entered, talking quietly.

Though most of the tables in the café were empty, Nate took a seat at the one beside theirs, putting him close to the principal.

"Heidi?"

She turned her head, interrupted in mid-sentence.

"I'm Nate Hollis, Edmund Bishop's uncle."

Her mouth, already open, widened, and surprise showed in her eyes. The woman with her reacted, too, plunking her coffee cup down in its saucer.

"Morris told me I could find you here."

He put a purposeful snark in his tone, a clear criticism of the break the principal was taking before the day had gotten far.

"After the kids are all inside, I come here for breakfast. You mind?"

"And you pay out of pocket every day, or on the school account's credit card?"

"It's Jacqueline," the other woman said. "Has to be."

"I don't know what she alleges, Mr…?"

"Hollis."

"You're Edmund's what?" the other woman asked. She had a light French accent and perfect teeth.

"Uncle. His father is my half-brother."

The woman went silent, her face contemplative, and Nate took a menu the waitress slipped him.

"Anyway," he said, looking back at the principal. "There's something upsetting Morris and Jacqueline."

"What doesn't upset Jackie?"

"Listen, you want to have this talk here? We can do that. But I'd think you'd want to talk in private."

The principal sighed, not all that fazed.

"Clotilde, excuse me. Give me a minute and I'll be right back."

Nate peeked over his shoulder as he walked away, struck by the somberness in Clotilde's pretty face.

***

"I didn't mail any threats to her."

Shock came from the principal's voice, whether feigned or real, and she took a deep breath to gather herself. A man walking by on the sidewalk had looked in her direction.

"I have a school to run. I don't threaten the parents with physical harm."

Nate had to admit that the way she stood her ground impressed him.

"And why are *you* coming to me? Jackie knows where my office is."

"I'm helping them out."

"I see," the principal said. "And what do you do – for your line of work?"

Nate ignored her question.

"So I can tell them, with confidence, that this'll stop? With your background, I don't think you want more trouble."

"What the hell does that mean?"

"Way I hear it, before coming here, you left PS 58 under a cloud. The Department of Ed is looking into stuff you did as a teacher there."

"We're done," the principal said. "I don't know who you think you are…"

She pulled at her sweater collar and spun on her heel, but then stopped.

"What's supposed to be my reason for doing this? To scare Jackie off the board?"

"You said it. Not me."

"That's nonsense."

The principal flushed, thick cheeks puffy. Waving a dismissive arm at Nate, she moved toward the café's door.

It opened and her friend walked out.

"Everything okay?" the friend said.

"Clotilde's on the board herself," the principal said, her voice booming again. "Like me, she's trying to make this school work."

"What happened?" Clotilde said.

"Maybe it's time for Jackie to do the same. Think about the

school and what we're trying to do, not herself."

The principal gestured at the door and tramped back inside. Nate was left standing on the sidewalk with Clotilde, posh in her heels and office attire, make-up impeccable.

"Tell Jackie hello," she said, rolling her eyes. "I'll see her at the next board meeting."

And then she returned to the café, and Nate felt the autumn wind biting through his jacket.

***

Nate found the case, if he could even call it that, to be a curious one. Nobody had been hurt, nobody was missing, and his co-clients were a divorced pair who got along amicably. He enjoyed staying with Morris in Brooklyn, sleeping on Mo's living room futon, bullshitting at night while drinking single malt Mo had bought – Laphroaig no less. They relived old times, Atlantic City. There had been the blackjack team and its temporary success, parties and women, the mysterious work, never specified, that Nate did for a well-heeled Jersey businessman gambler. Mo, like Nate, had fallen out of touch with the three other guys who were part of their short-lived card-counting venture, and Nate couldn't help but kid Mo over where he'd ended up.

"Married, divorced, a child, and best of all, you're a bureaucrat now."

"It's a steady paycheck, working for the City."

"Don't gotta tell me. My pop and grandfather did it."

"Whole lot different being a cop than working for the Department of Finance."

"I bet you deal with your share of angry people."

"Through correspondence. Not out in the street."

Nate chuckled. "And now it's you who's pissed," he said. "Far as the school goes."

From what he could piece together, Heidi Zanderlein was indeed bad news. Besides Mo and Jackie, a number of parents didn't come across as her fans. Nate had chatted with them in the afternoons, outside the school, when he accompanied Jackie to pick up Edmund under the guise of being the child's visiting uncle, and they had no qualms dishing dirt. With her own son and daughter enrolled at the French American Academy, she'd turned up and run for Parent Association president despite the grade fraud rumors surrounding her departure from the French English program at the public school twenty blocks away. She'd used her teaching experience as a selling point to the other parents. She knew the system, she said, and could use her knowledge on behalf of the parents and therefore the children.

What she'd proceeded to do, in every way she could, was make the first principal's life a living hell, some days following her around the school to observe whether everything the principal did followed Department of Education guidelines to the letter. Her calls and emails to the DOE – regarding a clogged bathroom toilet, a bedbug scare, brusqueness the principal used in addressing parents – had piled up to the point where the first principal, fed up, unable to focus on her job, had resigned under pressure from a hostile board Heidi lobbied. Midyear, and despite no background in administration, she'd convinced the board that she was the person who could fix the school's problems. But since they'd named her principal in a 5-2 vote (with Jacqueline one of the two voting against), those problems and new ones had wasted at least $300,000 on fees paid to educational consultants. Heidi and the board had brought them in to study the school's practices and make recommendations for changes. Then there were lawyers hired to handle suits from three teachers Heidi had dismissed, and who knew the sum they'd shelled out to pay an accounting and payroll service, retained because the board had let go the school's first operations director, an ally of the departed principal? As a member of the board, Jacqueline got to see the school's books, and all she could say is that they were a disaster.

"I don't know where to start," she said. "Maybe by going to the papers and spilling the beans?"

"On cooked books or waste?"

"Hard to tell," Jackie said. "Maybe both. Something's going on."

If she had told Heidi she'd go public, which she swore she hadn't, no wonder she'd gotten threats. But Mo and Jackie, Nate thought, had all their suspicions pointed at the principal, when the board's make-up said it could be somebody else. Including its chairman, six people now sat on the board, and five supported

Heidi. The man who had joined Jacqueline in voting against Heidi's selection as principal had quit the board. The other five, despite the school's continuing difficulties, claimed they believed she fostered stability after the school's rocky start. She was committed to the school long term, and they asserted that more parents than not backed Heidi. So the efforts to intimidate Jackie into stepping down could be coming from any of them.

That woman Clotilde, for instance, the chi-chi one with her straightened hair. How strange a look she'd given him when he'd entered the café. Would she deliver threats, that stylish exterior notwithstanding? He asked Mo about her and Mo shrugged. She and Jackie disagreed often on the board, he said, but he couldn't see her threatening Jackie with violence.

"Why not?" Nate asked. "She and Heidi were friendly when I saw them."

"She's got a kid in Edmund's third grade class. They play together."

"So?"

"I don't see it."

That told Nate nothing, and he decided to talk to Clotilde himself. Today was Saturday; he'd speak to her Monday. In the meantime, during the weekend, he hung with Mo and Edmund, who Mo came to get from afterschool every Friday evening. Though shy, the kid had a big sweet smile, and he didn't appear disturbed by the presence of a stranger in his dad's apartment.

"What do you think of the school?" Nate asked him.

"I like it."

They were at a pizza place, seated, having slices.

"Oh, the kids don't complain," Mo said.

"Maybe you should let the kids run it," Nate said. "Clear out the adults."

"Couldn't hurt."

Nate went with them to the movies Saturday night and later, he watched Mo tuck Edmund into bed. The kid had it good, despite his parents' split. Whether in Manhattan on weekdays or in Brooklyn on weekends, he got lavished with attention.

The ringing of a jangly land line phone woke Nate up Sunday morning, and he opened his eyes to hear someone shouting. The person was Morris, in his bedroom, voice frantic.

"Shit! Are you all right?"

Nate rolled from the futon and stepped across the living room, to Morris' doorway.

"Someone attacked Jackie just now."

From promised words to an actual deed – Morris was gaping at him, the cordless phone in his hand, his head shaking from side to side.

"Someone..."

"Who?"

"She doesn't know."

"In her house?" Nate asked.

"Outside in the park while she was running."

Nate had re-crossed the living room, and he opened the closet in the hall. He yanked a clean shirt and pants off the hangers.

"She sounds okay," Morris said. "But she's shaken up."

"Did she call the cops?"

Morris asked her.

"No," Morris said. "Not yet."

"Tell her to sit tight. I'm going over."

"We're going together."

"You should stay here with your son."

"Fuck, Nate!"

"It's better. I'll call you soon as I get there."

***

On her forearm she had a blue icepack, held in place by an elastic bandage. She said her attacker had rushed out of the bushes at the side of the path where she was jogging, a metal bar in her gloved hands. The overhand blow had been directed at her head – no doubt of that – but she'd been swift enough to raise her right arm and block it. Nobody was near and she'd yelled out, perhaps scaring her assailant away with the noise. In pain, still running, she'd returned home.

"You said *her*," Nate said.

"I think so. The track suit was baggy and she had a stocking over her face, but I could see enough of her shape, and the way the person moved – it had to be a woman."

"Heidi Zanderlein?"

Jacqueline shook her head. She hadn't changed out of her own running outfit, keeping on her t-shirt though she'd removed her zippered sweat jacket to apply the cold pack and bandage. She was trying to keep her arm stationary, extended on top of the kitchen table. But every time she moved in her chair, affecting the injured arm at all, her face screwed up in pain. She'd taken two tablets of ibuprofen, not that she expected them to help.

"It couldn't have been," she said. "Couldn't have. Heidi's bigger than that."

"You sure?"

"Positive. And there's no way" – she flashed a grim smile – "that Heidi could be that fast on her feet."

"What about Clotilde?"

"Clotilde? She's not my friend but – "

"Yeah?"

"Why're you askin' about her?"

"I met her the other day. Didn't like the feeling I got."

"She's Heidi's main ally on the board, along with the chairman, Phillipe, but it's not like I have any friends on it."

"You want to bring this to the cops? Make a report?"

"I should, shouldn't I?"

"Most people would."

"But you're saying I shouldn't?"

"Someone on the board did this," Nate said, "if not Heidi, and there's a public meeting Tuesday, right?"

"There is."

"Can you hold off till then?"

"What do you mean?"

"Make the assault public then. If you want to really make your point."

"But we don't know who did it."

"Don't accuse anyone," Nate said. "Just say what happened and that you think it could've been someone on the board. Unless you think that's too extreme."

Jackie's face lightened and a glint appeared in her eyes. "Hell, no. All hell might break loose, but no." She giggled then stopped, wincing.

"We'll see where the parents truly stand," she said. "Who's with Heidi, who's not."

"Where's Edmund going to be?"

"I'll get a sitter."

She said that Morris would hate the idea but she would tell him before Tuesday, to get him prepared.

"Why will he hate it?"

"For everything he says, he's not into confrontation. Shies away from it actually."

Nate thought back. What she said sounded accurate. Of the blackjack team members, Mo had been the low-key guy, betraying no emotion when he got blackjack or pulled a winning card, never deviating from the strict betting system they had. He'd been the best among them at not drawing the attention of the pit bosses.

"If I'm not overstepping," Nate said, "you two seem to get along well."

"I guess," Jackie said. "There's Edmund to consider. And we don't get in each other's hair. He has his life, I have mine."

It occurred to Nate that of all the shooting the shit they'd done, he and Mo hadn't discussed any women in their lives now, only women from the past. Mo hadn't mentioned anybody he was seeing, nor had he expressed any interest in what Nate might be doing on that front. Yet Mo spent Sunday night to Thursday night alone, and Nate couldn't believe that Mo lived like a monk.

Nate's cell phone buzzed and he took it out of his pocket.

Morris, who he'd forgotten to call.

"How is she, Nate?"

"She has a bruised arm."

"That's it?"

"Come over now. I'll wait."

Jackie nodded.

Nate put his phone in her hand so that the two could talk.

***

The night of the board meeting, Nate felt as if he was attending a UN convention. Mo and Jackie hadn't been kidding when they said that the parent body was diverse. From clothes, skin tones, and features, Nate saw what Mo had described as the Francophone world before him, people from anywhere French was the predominant language of the country. There were also the Anglo parents, black and white. Everyone had assembled in the school's cafeteria, the parents sitting on the benches attached to the long tables. The six board members, Heidi Zanderlein and the parent representative – a curly-haired Frenchwoman – faced the parents from behind school desks lined up for the occasion. Between this group and the parents was a wide stretch of light-blue floor, an expanse Nate had imagined laid with mines to protect board members from any parents who got so angry they wanted to rush them.

As it happened, it didn't take long for the fireworks to begin. No sooner had Phillipe, in his role as board chairman, declared the meeting open, than a woman stood up and lit into Heidi Zanderlein. She was tall and thin, with close-cropped kinky hair and dressed in jeans and a black sweat shirt. From her voice, Nate took her to be an American, an assumption supported by where she was sitting. In this school, apparently, segregation went by culture as well as region of origin. The West African parents, all in Western clothes except for a couple of the women, occupied their own table; white French-speaking parents another table and a half; and the native New York City residents still another. The divisions weren't perfect – a white Anglo guy sat at the black American table and a North African woman in the French zone – but the distinctions were obvious.

"So we're all clear," the standing woman was saying. "I'll be letting the Department of Ed know everything Heidi's doing here."

Phillipe, immaculate in a green suit with a red tie, sixtyish and bald but debonair in manner, smiled with a smoothness befitting a politician. He was, in fact, as Jackie had told Nate, the French government consular advisor for the New York metropolitan area. His tone carried a hint of superiority. Perhaps his English accent, an indication of where he'd learnt the language, added to this.

"There's no need for that," he said. "As I've stated before, our problems, such as they are, can and should be handled here. By all of us."

Heidi sat stoically behind her desk, gazing straight ahead. She was to the right of the board members, beside Clotilde.

"She's a menace to the children," the woman said.

"She's doing her job," Phillipe said. "If the principal sees certain signs, she's duty bound to call Child Services."

"Are you kidding me?" the woman asked. Her voice was rising. "I'm trying to keep this civil."

"Why?" somebody else said, the white guy in the American section. "They're not. Tell everyone what she does."

"Please," Phillipe said, casting a look at Heidi. "This is neither the time nor place."

"When is?" the man said. "Our wonderful principal calls Child Services on parents who she considers a pain to herself. That's what she's doing – point blank. How many times has she called on you, Gwen? And each time CS finds nothing."

Among the board members, Jackie sat with her hands folded on her desk, her expression placid. The way the meeting was going, would she even get an opening to announce the assault on herself? Still, she appeared to like the way things had kicked off, with Gwen launching her attack on the principal. And with Gwen's defender, broad-shouldered and burly, involved now, too, additional parents joined in though some spoke in Heidi's defense. The other board members, three men and two women, Clotilde included, were sitting stock still as the argument grew. Their faces didn't show unease. If anything, they looked bored, as if this rancor and accusatory talk, the people hollering and motioning, chiming in over one another, was typical of a public meeting at the school. Nate supposed it must be, and wondered what the damn kids would think to see their parents behaving like this.

"*S'il vouz plait*," Phillipe said, when a moment of silence somehow occurred and he got to interject a word. "This is not productive for us."

Clotilde then spoke for the first time, asking to be excused.

She rose.

"You have the nerve to leave?" Gwen said.

"I have to go to the bathroom," Clotilde said. "If I'm permitted by law to do that."

"You promise to come back?" someone said.

There was laughter.

The tension had eased, though Gwen remained standing. Nate wheeled around to look down his table at Mo, but didn't see him. He couldn't spot him anywhere in the cafeteria. When had he gone? Nate felt an itch, a prickling under his skin, and got up. He shot a glance at Jackie, whose eyes were on him, squinched and inquisitive, and left the cafeteria himself.

He went down a hall that passed a door labeled "Boys". He heard no movement inside the bathroom and none from the girls' room farther along. The hallway led to a stairwell climbing to the school's street level floor, and when he arrived up there, by the security guard's station and near the doors leading outside, he paused again and listened.

"I'm looking for my friend," he said.

"Sir?"

"Should've come up a second ago."

"Mr. Bishop?"

'Yes."

"He left."

Nate opened the iron door and stepped out onto the pavement. Nobody was on the block, but it was well-lit from the newly constructed apartment building across the street. East was Frederick Douglass Boulevard, a central thoroughfare with lots of activity. He hurried west toward Manhattan Avenue, a street more quiet with its string of brownstones. As he got near the corner, he could hear raised voices, and sure enough he recognized Mo's. Then on Manhattan he saw them both, about half a block away, and he stopped in his tracks to watch.

If Mo disliked confrontation, Nate couldn't tell: his friend was embroiled in an argument now. Clotilde in her skirt, stockings and heels, no coat despite the cold, was laying into him, and Morris was trying to talk over her. Their body language said it all.

Well, judging by her looks alone, Mo's decision was comprehensible.

Goddamn, Mo.

Nate debated whether to cut in. Let them know he knew. He felt he should – Morris deserved that – but he thought of Jackie back at the meeting. She was about to make her revelation, if she hadn't already, and he saw no need for her to do it anymore. Why add to the poor school's turmoil?

He ducked back around the edge of a building and returned up the block to the blue entrance doors.

In the cafeteria, discussion had become heated again. He re-entered to find a heavyset woman in a flowing blue and orange dress at the African table haranguing the board and Heidi. It didn't take Nate long to figure out she was a teacher Heidi had recently fired. Of the three she had sacked, two were African, leaving the school with twelve white instructors and two of color.

She was calling the dismissal a racist act.

"If this keeps up, we'll have to have people removed," Phillipe said. "The board has business to get to and votes to take."

He was frowning but calm, a hammer wrapped in silk.

"How?" the former teacher demanded. "You going to call the police?"

"I'd like to see you do that," somebody yelled.

"Can you stop?" a man with a French accent said. "You're ruining this meeting for everyone else and some of us have lives. We have to get home before the night ends."

"Then go," the ex-teacher said. "You can leave."

"I'm not leaving. I came to hear about the school's finances and test scores. We need to hear that."

"*You* do."

"That's right," said Gwen, back in the thick of it. "You're not the one who lost a job or who they call Child Services on."

Nate had sat down and made eye contact across the room with Jackie. He dipped his head and slowly ran his hand across his throat, trying to communicate the need for silence, that she shouldn't say what he'd told her to say. He could see confusion pinch her face but she seemed to understand, and soon afterwards, her husband came back, re-seating himself beside Nate.

"You can't vote on anything anyhow," the beefy guy at the Harlem table said. "Not till Clotilde gets here."

Clotilde didn't return, and after more arguing among everybody – Phillipe, even Heidi, the separate parental cliques – Gwen brought this fact to the meeting's attention.

"You talk about arrogance. She flat out bolted."

"*Je ne suis pas surprise,*" a woman's voice said, from the African table. "She doesn't like what we were saying so she left."

"It's normal for this school," said Gwen. "That attitude."

Phillipe stood, his face red, teeth showing on his upper lip, and proclaimed that the meeting was over.

"If we can't act like civilized people…"

"Clotilde can't have left," said Heidi. "Her bag's still here."

And it was, the strap slung over the back of the chair she'd occupied.

"Maybe she fell ill," Jackie said.

Genuine concern sounded in her voice, and Nate looked at Mo, who gave away nothing. Mo had risen, and was putting on his black pea coat.

"I'll go check the lady's room," said Heidi.

She headed out, light on her feet for a person her size, and people began talking and grumbling among themselves, a cacophony of French and English. Parents were standing up, either collecting themselves to go or waiting for Heidi to walk back in. She reappeared after minutes had passed, and at once she said she'd searched every bathroom. She'd gone to all three floors.

No Clotilde.

More chatter ensued and Nate grabbed his jacket. Morris slid past him as Jackie walked around the line of desks and approached them both, and Nate heard her say, "Wonder what happened?"

"Damned if I know," Morris said.

"Didn't you go out, too?"

"For a call I had to make. I didn't see her."

Nate felt he had listened to enough and took a step over to them.

"She's probably okay," he said, speaking as softly as he could in the noise. He was staring at Mo. "Right, Mo? She's probably okay but doesn't want to show her face right now."

"What are you talking about?"

"Let's get out of here," said Nate. "Go to a bar and have a drink."

"I could use one," Jackie said.

"I'll bet."

"Let's go then," said Mo.

His eyes on Nate, he edged away, and his face remained set and inscrutable.

"I need to talk to y'all," Nate said.

***

There'd been no physical violence between Mo and Clotilde, a relief to Nate. Once he knew that, he spoke to Jackie alone, at her apartment, and he spelled out how the assault gave her leverage.

"May as well use it," Nate said, and she liked what she heard. She said she'd phone Phillipe and set up a meeting. And mark her words: Phillipe *would* meet with her, and he'd do it without Heidi or another board member present.

They got together in Phillipe's office, high above Madison Avenue. Bright sunlight shone through the glass panes, and Nate could see Queens across the East River. In his day job, when not fulfilling his consular duties for French citizens living in the City, Phillipe was a corporate lawyer specializing in litigation.

"So what can I do for you?" he said, sheltered behind his enormous desk. He had the classic attorney's office, with leather armchairs, a carpet, a bookcase, and framed degrees on the wall behind his swivel chair.

Nate took it in, unimpressed, though he'd worn a jacket for the talk. After he introduced himself, he got right into negotiating on Jackie's behalf.

"You sound like you're her lawyer," Phillipe said, smiling blandly. Today his tailored suit was cobalt blue, his tie green. He had a handkerchief in his breast pocket. "She didn't say she was coming with a lawyer."

"I'm here to help," Nate said, poker-faced.

Phillipe fidgeted in his chair but kept the smile on his face. "Help how? Intimidation I don't respond to."

"Who's talking intimidation?" Jackie said. "Nate's the person who helped me after the attack and who saw Clotilde and Morris together. I want him here so there's no misunderstandings about what transpired."

"I think we know what transpired."

"Glad we agree."

"I've told Clotilde she has to step down from the board."

"And did she?"

"She's out," Phillipe said. "It's done."

"Least she can do," Nate said.

"Was filing a report necessary? Having her arrested?"

"She attacked me, Phillipe," Jackie said, agitated.

"I know that but –"

"Is that the publicity the school wants?"

"What she did wasn't about the school."

"Wasn't it?" Nate said, interjecting himself into the exchange.

"We know it wasn't."

"The attack might've been about getting rid of a sworn opponent on the board."

"That's insane," Phillipe said. "She and Jackie's husband…Ex-husband…"

"Call it what you will," Nate said. "But a story in the *Post*. Parent attacking parent. Would that help the school?"

"Naturally not."

"Then why go there?"

"And she's still a parent," Jackie said. "I still have to see her and hope she doesn't do something to my kid."

"I can't throw her out of the school. We're not private and there's due process. If you pursue the charges and the case gets to court – "

"We'll worry about that," Nate said. "The bigger issue here is whether you'll do what Jackie asked about Heidi."

Phillipe looked at Jackie, at Nate, back at Jackie.

"You do know what you're doing is extortion."

"We're asking you," Jackie said, "to hire an experienced principal. Someone the parents and teachers can respect."

"We couldn't please every parent with any principal."

"They're a tough crowd," Jackie acknowledged. "But we need someone who doesn't play favorites among the particular groups."

"You can't prove she's done that."

"Do you want to the school to succeed or don't you?"

Phillipe waved his hand. "We've all put our time and sweat into it."

"*Alors*. What's the issue? She's running the place into the ground."

"You're position on the board forbids you from revealing financial information about the school – just a reminder."

"And I'm reminding you that the finances are a mess and need to be cleaned up. I'm reminding you that Heidi's misuse of school money, spending it on herself, besides her other shenanigans – the threats to parents, the overall ineptitude from lack of experience – would also make great newspaper copy."

Phillipe closed his eyes. He had his interlocked fingers under his chin. He might've been ransacking his brain for a miracle plan to end the crisis on his terms, but nothing in his face or posture suggested that he came up with anything.

"It'll take time to find a replacement," he said, eyes open again. "We never even filled the vice principal spot."

"You can do it," Jackie said. "I have faith in you."

***

"Thank you," said Jackie, when she and Nate were out in the corridor, waiting for the elevator. "It was worth it to see that smug bastard squirm."

"I hope the changes help the school."

"They will," she said. "Those two gone? It's a start."

"You're determined. I'll grant you that."

"With the mix of people, it could be a great place. I'm not quite ready to give up on it."

A bell rang and the elevator doors opened.

***

Nate said a cab would do, but Morris insisted on driving him to the airport.

"I'm sorry," Mo said, once they were out on the highway. "I had no idea the threats were from her."

"I believe that," Nate said. "Happens when you don't use your brain for your thinking."

"All too true."

"It didn't bother you that she and Jackie never agree on board matters."

"I thought I could keep the school stuff and the other separate."

"So stand with your ex on school stuff, and in public, but fuck Clotilde in private."

"Clotilde was fine with it. Or I thought she was."

Nate felt bad for Edmund, who'd become aware quickly of the drop in civility between his parents.

"You think it'll go to trial?" Mo asked.

"Is there a need? Any halfway decent lawer'll have her take a plea."

"Hope so, for everyone involved."

"I'm more worried about Jackie. She's got to see Clotilde."

"She has the order of protection."

"Still got to see her at the school."

"I doubt Clotilde will keep her kid there. She's persona non grata with practically everyone."

"That's rough for her kid. She didn't do anything wrong."

When they reached the terminal at La Guardia, Nate took his suitcase and got out. Their handshake on the sidewalk, by the curbside check-in area, was perfunctory.

"If you're ever in New York again…"

"Sure," Nate said. "I'll let you know."

Mo jumped back into the car and drove off. Nate watched his old friend go, feeling a vague sense of sadness. Then he checked his bag.

THE PARACHUTE KIDS

by

Sarah M. Chen

Run, run, run.

The girl ran as fast as she could past the swimming pool for the side gate. Her arms and legs still hurt from the fight last week. It was three against one, but she did good. Ornj said so.

Fat pig! That's what had started it. She knew what that meant, and wasn't going to let the boy call her that. Not anymore.

Ppalli-ppalli, ppalli-ppalli.

Faster, faster.

His shoes pounded on the pavement behind her. The girl turned around. She could see his eyes, like angry fire. She dropped the heavy bag. There, that was better.

At first, America was a beautiful fairy tale. Her *appa* was right. Blue cloudless skies every day. Clean air that filled her lungs with sunshine and hope. Not like back home in Seoul.

But her *appa* didn't tell her that nobody would like her. That mean rich kids would make fun of her. That she had nobody to help her.

Until she met Ornj.

Ppalli-ppalli, ppalli-ppalli.

Faster, faster.

"Sunny!" A strong hand grabbed her arm and yanked her back. She struggled to free herself. She kicked him in the leg and he howled. Good.

"You bitch!" He hit her hard—*whack!*—across the face and she staggered backwards until she fell, her head striking something hard. An explosive pain the last thing she felt.

"*Je-song hamnida, appa,*" she whispered.

I am sorry, father.

***

Nate Hollis sat at the worn oak bar and took a swig of sweet tea. The lunch rush was over, with only a bickering young couple occupying a two-top in the corner. The bar's phone rang and his grandfather, Obadiah "Clutch" Hollis, walked over and answered, "Hideaway." He looked at Nate and nodded. "Uh-huh. He's here."

Nate ran through a list of people he didn't feel like talking to. The list was long.

"Just a second." His grandfather put the receiver down and looked at Nate. "It's a job. Said you're not answering your cell."

Nate reached into his pants pocket and pulled his phone out. Sure enough, there were two voicemail messages. He grabbed the receiver from Clutch's outstretched hand. "Nate Hollis here."

"Mr. Hollis. You're a hard man to get a hold of." The female voice was clipped.

"Who is this?"

"It's best if you come out here. As soon as possible. I'll give you the address."

"Hold on a sec, slow down." The heat was making him irritable. Los Angeles was having an unseasonable January heat wave. High eighties in downtown. "How'd you get my info?"

"From Bang Mi-Cha. Or you probably know her as Misha."

It took Nate a few seconds to realize she meant Misha Bang, Johnny Bang's wife. Johnny and Nate crossed paths every now and then, usually at Johnny's nightclub, The Summit, where he ruled Koreatown's streets. Johnny was born in South Korea, but L.A. was his home turf.

"Okay. What's the job?" Nate asked.

She insisted everything would be explained when he arrived. Nate wrote down the address. Rowland Heights. San Gabriel Valley. One hour. Ask for Joe Lee.

After hanging up, Nate immediately dialed a number on his cell phone. Johnny answered on the first ring.

"Yo, Hollis." Nate could hear pop music blasting in the background.

"Been a long time, my brother."

"That it has. That it has." Nate heard him exhale like he was smoking a cigarette. "You'll be gettin' a call about a job."

"Already did."

"This woman and Misha go to the same church. Korean Baptist up on Vermont. She and Misha got to talkin' about a girl who got killed. One of those parachute kids."

"Okay." Nate was familiar with the term. Parachute kids came from China, Korea, and Taiwan. Their parents paid big bucks to send their kids to American schools.

Bang continued, "It sounds like the cops are fingering the wrong people for this girl's murder. Misha recommended you."

Nate drummed his fingers on the bar. Caught Clutch's curious stare. "Okay, I'll check it out."

"Let me know how it goes." A pause. "Misha will be asking."

"I hear you." Nate had met Misha only once, but that was enough to know it wasn't a good idea to disappoint her. "Later, Johnny."

"Peace."

***

Rowland Heights was referred to by some as New Chinatown, due to the mass influx of Chinese immigrants in the late '70s and early '80s. Nate drove by noodle shops, acupuncture clinics, and karaoke bars. Signs in Chinese as well as English, with a few in Korean.

Nate could feel the curious stares as he put on his trilby and made his way to a dingy-looking one-story office next door to a Korean BBQ restaurant. The sign "American Cultural Education" had Korean lettering right above it.

The blast of air conditioning was shocking at first, then welcoming. The smell of mildew lingered in the air. A large banner covered the back wall. It read "American Cultural Education – Bringing Education to the World," with a group of people standing by an important-looking building. A sea of Asian faces with the exception of one or two. He wondered which one was Joe Lee. Probably the old man in the center shaking the hand of a beautiful Asian woman.

"Mr. Hollis. I'm Jo Lee."

Nate turned around to see the same beautiful Asian woman he had been ogling two seconds ago standing beside him in tailored pants and a sleeveless blouse. She was even more striking in person, with her high cheekbones and sharp inquisitive eyes.

"Is something wrong?" She looked amused.

"No, I uh…I was expecting somebody different," he admitted.

"That's funny. So was I."

They stared at each other until Nate chuckled. "Fair enough."

She led him to a small office where they both sat down. "Okay, down to business." She opened up a folder on her desk. "This girl was killed. I need you to find out who did it." She slid a photo toward Nate. "Her name was Kim Sun-mi. She went by Sunny. Her body was found two days ago."

Nate picked up the photo. It was a headshot, like a school photo, of an Asian girl. Maybe sixteen, seventeen. Slightly chubby. She looked resentful, like she didn't want her picture taken. "What happened?"

"The Reynolds, that's her host family, contacted ACE. Told me she never came home Monday night. Early the next morning, a jogger found her body in the field behind the school."

"So you set her up with the host family. ACE is like the middleman."

Jo nodded. "Exactly. We arrange for high school students in China, Korea, and Taiwan to attend school in Southern California and stay with local families. The students learn English and American culture. The host families learn about customs in foreign countries. It's a win-win for everyone."

Everyone except Sunny, Nate thought. "What do the police have?" He remembered Johnny mentioned something about the cops pinning it on the wrong people. "They arrest someone?"

Jo shook her head. "No, but I know they're going to. They've already brought them in for questioning."

"Who?"

"Three students. They're also with ACE. Two sisters, Jenny and Trin are their American names. Last name is Cheng. From an excellent family in Shanghai. The boy is Alex Wong." Her face tightened. "They're good kids."

"The police must have something on them. Why bring them in?"

She shifted in her seat and looked away from Nate. "I don't know. That's what I want you to find out."

Nate could tell she was hiding something. "Look, Ms. Lee, the police will find who killed Sunny. You don't need me."

Jo gripped the chair armrests. "You don't understand. Murrieta PD will arrest these kids because they're foreigners. They won't look anywhere else."

"Wait, did you say Murrieta?" Shit. That was way the hell out there in the IE. Near San Diego practically. And hot as hell.

She leaned forward, trapping Nate in her gaze. "Her father is flying here in three days to take his dead daughter back home with him to Korea. I have to show him some progress on this."

Nate raised his eyebrows. "So *that's* what this is. A show for the grieving father. ACE goes above and beyond for their clients when they get killed."

Jo Lee stared at Nate with hard eyes. "Does it really matter why, Mr. Hollis? A girl is dead." She slid over a letter-sized envelope stuffed with bills. "Here, I think this should cover your expenses for now."

Nate glanced inside. He wouldn't have to avoid his landlord this month. He stuffed the envelope inside his jacket pocket and stood up. "I'll be in touch, Ms. Lee."

He figured he'd poke around for a couple days until the police arrested the three kids. Then that'd be it. Show would be over.

***

The next day was even hotter than yesterday. After grabbing a quick breakfast, he jumped in his restored emerald green '69 Dodge Dart, heading east on the 91 to the 15 Freeway for Murrieta—a small commuter town of track homes in between Lake Elsinore and Pechanga Casino.

The Reynolds lived in a quiet neighborhood of wide streets and Southwestern-style houses with tiled roofs. He parked in front of their massive two-story home and climbed out of his car, putting his hat on. The sun beat down on him like a caged animal. It had to be close to ninety-five degrees. It was barely 10am.

Margie Reynolds, pale and thin with red-rimmed eyes, fluttered around nervously while her husband, who looked like a former linebacker, stared at Nate with suspicion. Probably the first time he had a black man standing in his living room.

Nate wrote down all the information they gave him: her school schedule, bus route, teachers. Her backpack and cell phone were missing. When Nate asked who Sunny's friends were, the Reynolds looked at each other. Margie spoke first.

"She had a tough time here initially. She seemed really lonely so I took her places to cheer her up. My bible study group. And church every Sunday."

Bet that was a lot of laughs for the kid, Nate thought.

"Then—oh, I don't know, about two months ago—things changed. She went out more often. She seemed happier."

"Where'd she hang out?" Nate asked.

"Well, I..." Margie's hand went to her chest. She looked to Larry.

Larry cleared his throat. "We figured as long as she was happy, everything was fine."

Meaning they had no idea and didn't care. "So you don't know where she was Monday night," Nate said.

Margie flushed red. "I was in San Diego visiting my sister until Tuesday." She looked at Larry.

Larry visibly tensed. He looked to Margie, then Nate. "What? I had to work late. It's crunch time at the office. End of quarter sales. By the time I got home, I was exhausted and went straight to bed."

Great. This kid could stay out all night if she wanted. She could have gone anywhere. "What do you do?" Nate asked.

"Larry's the director of purchasing at Synatech," Margie said proudly.

Nate had no idea what that was, but it sounded as exciting as a root canal.

"Look, you need to stop interrogating us and look into those kids," Larry said, his voice rising. He glared at Nate, his fists clenching. "You're wasting time."

"What kids?" Nate wondered if it was the same kids Jo Lee mentioned.

"Those chinks who beat up Sunny," Larry said.

"Honey!" Margie exclaimed. "That's not very nice!"

Larry threw up his hands. "I'm sorry, but that's what they are.

They're no-good spoiled brats who think they can come into our country and do whatever the fuck they want."

"Larry!" Margie looked like she was ready to cry.

"Open your eyes, Margie. They murdered Sunny. They should be called a lot worse than chinks." Larry glowered at Nate. "They all had detention because of a fight at school last week. Sunny said they were calling her names and pushing her around. I told Detective Stevens all this too."

"You have their names?"

"I wrote them down." Margie disappeared to the back, her high heels echoing in the cavernous house.

There was an awkward silence as Larry scowled at Nate.

"I'll need to see her room," Nate said.

"What for? There's nothing in there. I checked."

"Coming from a guy who has no clue who Sunny's friends are or where she hangs out, that means jack shit to me."

Larry reddened. "Fine. But it's a waste of time."

"Yeah, you mentioned that."

Nate followed Larry up the sweeping staircase to the second floor. A glittering chandelier that had to weigh more than Nate's Dart hung from the ceiling. Sunny's room was at the end of the hall. It was tidy with nothing on the walls but a cross. A prison cell would be less depressing.

Nate sorted through her stuff but found nothing of interest. No journal or diary. No love notes tucked underneath the bed. He gazed out her window, a clear view of the Reynolds' backyard with a fire pit and Olympic-sized pool surrounded by paving stones and gravel.

"Look, I don't know why ACE hired a—" Larry paused. "Someone like you, but you're wasting your time talking to us."

Nate turned around to see the big man glowering at him.

"I'm beginning to think any conversation with you is a waste of my time." Nate held his stare. "Now why don't you get in your Range Rover or your BMW and go to your cubicle so I can do my job without you mouthin' off every five seconds?"

Larry turned a deep shade of purple. "You goddamned son of a bitch." Nate thought they were going to go at it right then, which was fine with him—he wanted to throw the asshole out the window—but Margie appeared in the doorway.

"Honey, what's going on?"

Larry gave Nate one last glare before turning around and stomping out of the room. "I gotta get to work."

Nate smiled at the flustered woman. "You have those names, Mrs. Reynolds?"

She nodded and handed a slip of paper to him. They were the same ones Jo Lee had given him. "I told ACE about the kids too."

Nate stuffed the paper in his pocket and said he'd be in touch. He walked outside into the blazing heat just in time to see Larry zoom down the driveway in a shiny black Range Rover. He looked over—caught Nate's smug grin—and gunned it down the street.

***

Fernwood Christian Academy was a sprawling campus with green grass and low cinderblock buildings. Banners hung on light posts proclaiming "We Are Teammates" and "We Are One."

After leaving the Reynolds, Nate had rung Jo Lee. He wanted to know why she'd made it sound like the Chinese kids were saints. She admitted she didn't want Nate to be biased and maybe not take the job. She swore she had no reason to hide anything else from him. She told him Fernwood Academy was waiting for him, and he could talk to the students himself.

When he walked into the administration office, the gray-haired receptionist, Mrs. Pool, said she'd go fetch the three students. Nate called Wesley, his contact at the L.A. County Coroner, while he waited.

"Hollis, how's it hanging?"

"Mostly to the left," Nate replied. That got him a chuckle. "Listen, man, I need a favor. You got anyone out in Riverside County? I need some info on a girl. Killed couple days ago." Nate gave him Sunny's details and the detective working the case.

"Yeah, I may know a guy. I'll see what I can do."

"Thanks, man, I owe you."

"You said that last time."

"You keeping count?"

"As a matter of fact, I am."

"Keep it up. Good practice for you."

Nate heard a snort before the call ended. Mrs. Pool returned with three Chinese teenagers in tow—two heavily-made up girls, and a boy whom Nate assumed was Alex. They all wore the gray and maroon school uniforms and stared at Nate with flat expressions.

"In here," Mrs. Pool said.

Nate followed Mrs. Pool and the kids to a break room. It smelled of stale coffee and disinfectant. The girls threw their designer purses onto a foldout table and sat, pulled out their cell phones and began texting. The boy leaned back in his chair and spread his legs out. His stare an outright challenge to Nate.

Another Chinese student walked in wearing the school uniform. She wore glasses and no make-up, making her look much younger. She smiled shyly at Nate.

"This is Lisa Chu," Mrs. Pool said. "She's an international student too, but her English is excellent." She nodded at Nate. "Well, I'll leave you to it." The receptionist walked out, the door slightly ajar.

Through Lisa's translations, Trin admitted to the fight with Sunny in the cafeteria last week, but Sunny started it.

Yeah, I bet, Nate thought.

Trin was the one who did all the talking. Jenny never looked up from her cell phone and Alex mad dogged Nate the entire time. On Monday, they hung out at the Promenade after school until about five p.m. and then drove around. They never saw Sunny.

"What's the Promenade?"

"The mall," Lisa said. "That is a popular place for hanging out."

"Is that where Sunny hangs out?"

Lisa translated and Trin shrugged. Nate sighed. This was a waste of time.

"Anything else you can tell me about Sunny?"

"*Bangzi*," Alex said.

Nate looked to Lisa. "What'd he say?"

She looked embarrassed. "It means 'long stick.' It's not a very nice term for Koreans. It's like saying someone is stupid like wood."

Nate pointed at Alex. "You keep it up, that's fine by me. I'll just let the cops take you down for Sunny's murder, how about that?"

Alex grinned. "Fat pig," he said. The sisters giggled. Then the boy grabbed his crotch. "Suck my dick."

Nate leaped up and flung the cheap table aside so he was towering over the boy. The girls jumped up, but Alex remained seated, glaring up at Nate with blatant hostility. Arms crossed in front of him.

Nate leaned down, getting right in Alex's face. "I hope you get arrested and thrown in prison because you know what? A punkass bitch like you won't even last one day." If he wasn't a minor, Nate would have picked the kid up and slammed him into the table. Nate he turned to leave, then pointed at the scowling teen. "And I know you understand me, asshole."

As Nate stormed out of the break room, he grabbed Jenny's cell phone out of her hand and tossed it on the floor. He passed by Mrs. Pool, who stood up from behind her desk.

"Everything okay? I thought I heard noise in there," she said.

"Could be rats. I'd call an exterminator," Nate said.

He interviewed Sunny's teachers as quickly as he could in case Mrs. Pool called security on him. None of them knew who could have killed Sunny, and nobody saw her after school Monday. They did say that Sunny had been a model student until the past month, when she started skipping classes. They sent letters to her host family but got no response.

He went to the field behind the school where Sunny's body was found. It was about the length of a football stadium with nothing but dirt and yellowing grass. The crime scene tape marked off a large area of overgrown dry brush. He poked around but found nothing.

Nate headed back to his car, feeling like the heat cranked up another twenty degrees.

"Mr. Hollis!"

He turned around to see Lisa Chu running across the school parking lot toward him, her long black hair waving back and forth behind her. He stopped, waited for her to catch her breath.

"Hey, Miss Chu, thanks for helping me today. Sorry about the outburst."

"I understand. They aren't very nice." She giggled. "It was funny to see Alex's face."

"Do you think they killed Sunny?"

She pursed her lips and shrugged. "They're awful, but I don't know if they would kill someone. But you never know what people will do."

Nate nodded. "Did you know Sunny?"

Lisa bit her lip. "That's what I want to tell you. Just not in there."

"Okay."

"Sunny and I used to hang out sometimes. I felt sorry for her. But then we stopped about a month ago. She became like a different person. She cut class. Shaved her head on one side."

The Reynolds never mentioned that, Nate thought. Probably didn't notice.

"One day, I saw Sunny get into a car I'd never seen before," Lisa continued. "I remember thinking it was strange because she always walked or took the bus."

"What'd the car look like?" Nate pulled out his notepad.

"It was small. Like a Honda or Toyota. And blue. But it was like a sports car. And short."

"Short?"

She put her hand out, palm down, and bent her knees. "Close to the ground."

Lowrider.

"And loud."

"This is good stuff, Miss Chu. Anything else? Driver? Plate?" Nate scribbled everything down.

She shook her head. "Sorry. The windows were dark. I don't remember the plate."

"Did you tell the police?" he asked.

Her face tightened. "No. In my country, we don't trust the police."

"But you trust me."

She nodded. "I know you will find who killed Sunny."

Nate hoped she was right. He gave her his card and said to call him if she remembered anything else.

As he climbed into his Dart, he spotted Trin, Jenny, and Alex lounging by a black Mercedes sedan a few aisles over. They stared at Nate. Nate watched them from his rearview as he pulled away, heading out of the lot.

***

The Riverside County Coroner was in Perris, about twenty minutes away off the 215 Freeway. Nate walked by a beat-up junker as he headed to the coroner's building and the driver's side door swung open, almost hitting him. A heavy-set man in his mid-fifties climbed out. He looked like he just rolled out of bed.

"You Nate Hollis?"

"Frank Benson?"

The man nodded. His gray hair stuck up in tufts, with most of it plastered to his temple with sweat.

"Figured it was you. Get in," he said.

Nate didn't like the idea of getting in the guy's car, but figured he could take him if he had to. He got in, leaving the door open for air. It stank of stale fast food and dirty socks. He kicked a pile of trash away to rest his feet on the floor.

"Can't we go somewhere air conditioned?" Nate asked.

"Look at you, Miss Princess." The guy shook his head. "You want this info or not? I'm not taking you inside. I'd like to keep my job." He coughed and opened his door, spit onto the pavement. "I'm only doing you this favor because Wesley and I used to work together in L.A. Came out to this shithole because of the old lady. Wanted to be close to her dying sister." He snorted. "The fucking sister hasn't died yet. Been six years and I'm still here."

"What you got?"

The guy handed him a manila envelope. "See if that doesn't get your rocks off."

Nate tipped the envelope upside down and the coroner's report and photos fell into his lap. Nate picked up the report, scanning through it.

"Cause of death is an extradural hematoma," Frank said.

Nate nodded. "Bleeding of the brain."

"Looks like she struck the back of her head on something hard," Frank continued. "There's no telling how long she suffered. Probably not long."

Nate skimmed more of the details while Frank jabbered away.

"She was punched in the left side of her face. With considerable force, too. It fractured her jaw. Time of death looks to be anywhere from four to six."

That still means the three Chinese kids could have done it, Nate thought. They were at the mall until five, but no alibi after that. Only problem was none of them looked strong enough to fracture someone's jaw with one punch. Maybe Alex could. He was enough of an asshole to do it.

"Of course, her body was moved. She wasn't killed in that field."

"Oh?" Nate thought about that. The three kids could easily move a body. Throw her in the trunk of their Mercedes, dump her out in the field.

"Any ideas where she was killed?"

Frank shrugged. "We've got some pebbles stuck in the treads of her shoes and soil deposits on her clothes. A few gray carpet fibers."

Nate turned his attention to the crime scene photos, Sunny from various angles. She was sprawled out on the dry grass, her arms and legs flung haphazardly like a child's discarded doll. She wore her school uniform, a pleated skirt and polo shirt. Like Lisa said, her hair was spiky short.

There were dark marks all over her arms and legs. Nate pointed. "What about these?"

"Those are bruises. At least a week old, maybe more." Frank shifted in his seat. The springs groaned. "I hear she got into a big fight at school. That's probably what it's from."

Nate came to a photo that was a close-up of Sunny's head. He peered closer. "These look like cigarette burns." He pointed to two small dark circles behind her left ear. They were in a diagonal pattern.

Frank leaned over, smelling of something sour. "You got it."

"Recent?"

He shook his head. "Nah, maybe a couple months old. Tissue is already scarring and toughening up." He looked at Nate. "Possibly from another fight at school. We found one more burn in between her hallux and the long toe."

"Big toe and second toe."

Frank nodded. "Could have been self-inflicted. Fuckin' teenagers do crazy shit." He shook his head. "Got a twelve-year-old at home. Already acting like a diva who hates the world."

"Can I have this?" Nate held up the photo with the burns.

Frank hesitated.

"Look, man. My client thinks I'm not doing shit on this case. I show her this and she'll be happy." Nate smiled.

Frank sighed. "Sure. It's just a copy." He shrugged. "Won't do much good anyway. I hear they've got search warrants for those three kids."

Nate would have been fine with those three punks getting arrested, but Sunny's killer was still out there.

***

While driving back to L.A. on the 10 Freeway, the setting sun in his eyes the entire way, Nate received a call. It was Lisa Chu.

"I remembered something else," she said.

"Shoot."

"Excuse me?"

"What is it?"

"She wrote something on her folder. Over and over. During class. I think it stands for something."

"Okay." Nate scrambled for a pen and notepad while keeping one hand on the wheel.

"O-R-N-J."

Nate wrote it down. "These initials mean anything to you?"

"No."

"Okay, this is good. Thanks, Lisa. You've been a big help."

By the time, Nate exited the 10 Freeway and headed up to K-Town, it was almost seven. He drove down Wilshire Blvd. past tri-level mini-malls, parking garages, and high-rise office buildings. He left his car with the valet, saying he'd be right back, and entered The Summit, Johnny Bang's nightclub.

Nate waited for his eyes to adjust to the dim light before threading his way through the tables to the bar. It was early so the club was empty except for the bartender prepping for the night. The Asian girl with the fake tits in the tight tank top frowned at him.

"We're not open yet," she said.

"I'm here to see Johnny. He upstairs?"

She nodded. Nate walked past the small DJ booth and climbed the stairs to the second floor. He walked down the hall to where two large Korean men with shaved heads stood on either side of a doorway wearing tight T-shirts and baggy pants. They looked at Nate, expressionless.

"I'm here to see Johnny," Nate said. "Nate Hollis."

Nate raised his arms, and one guy patted him down quickly. Nate knew not to bother bringing his piece. The other knocked once on the door and opened it.

Nate walked in and Johnny stood up from behind his desk. The lean Korean man wore a button down shirt with the sleeves rolled up, revealing tats up and down his arms. He stretched out his hand.

"Hollis, my man."

They shook hands and Johnny gestured to a chair in front of the desk. "Have a seat."

Nate sat down and watched Johnny pull out a cigarette from a pack and light it. He held the box out to Nate. Nate shook his head and looked around. The office was cluttered with stacks of papers and files. Just as it was five years ago. "How's Misha and the kids?"

Johnny sat and stretched back in his chair. He eyed Nate through a cloud of smoke. "They're fine. Girls are in fourth grade now. How's the case?"

"It's why I'm here."

"I figured." He nodded. "Tell me what you got."

Nate gave him a brief rundown on Sunny and the Chinese kids the cops were hot to arrest.

"But you don't think they did it," Johnny said.

Nate shook his head. "The kids are assholes, but I think Sunny got hooked up with a gang."

Johnny raised his eyebrows. Nate pulled out the manila envelope from the inside of his jacket. He pulled out the photo of Sunny with the cigarette burns, slid it to Johnny.

Johnny leaned forward, peered at the photo. He whistled. "Girl got marked all right."

"There's one in between her big toe and second toe too."

Johnny took a long drag from his cigarette. He squinted through the smoke at Nate. "Murrieta, you say?"

Nate nodded.

"Could be those Chinese kids burned her during the fight. Held her down," Johnny said.

"But you don't believe that," Nate said.

"You don't want to stir up trouble and have it turn out to be wrong."

Nate leaned forward. "I've got an eyewitness who saw Sunny climb into a tricked-out tuner. And she wrote this all over her school folder." Nate pulled out the piece of paper he wrote "ORNJ" on, placing it in front of Johnny.

Johnny glanced down at it. His face displayed no emotion.

"I know you know what this means," Nate said.

They locked eyes for what felt like an hour until Johnny sighed. "You'll get to them eventually. I know you. You're so fucking stubborn." He put out his cigarette. "The Korean Klan or KK. They're an offshoot of the Killaz out here. These guys are a bunch of kids who think they're hot shit." He also leaned forward. "But that don't mean you shouldn't take them seriously. Kidnapping, home invasions in the OC and the IE. That's the shit they're into." His finger tapped the paper with "ORNJ" written on it. "Orange is the one you want."

"Orange?"

Johnny nodded. "O-R-N-J. Hair's dyed a fucked-up ugly orange color. Thinks it makes him a tiger. Tigers are a sign of power in Korea."

"How do I find this cat?"

"I hear he hangs out at one of those booking clubs. The Pegu. Out in Anaheim."

"Booking club? Like a strip club?"

Johnny shook his head. "You'll see."

Nate stood and shook Johnny's hand. "Thanks, my brother."

"You watch your back, Hollis."

Nate gave him a salute as he walked out. "Always do."

***

The Hideaway was hopping by the time Nate arrived. The regulars nodded at him as he grabbed a seat at the bar.

Clutch walked over, threw down a cocktail napkin, plopped a longneck down.

"You look like you could use this. Tough day?"

"You have no idea, grandpa."

110

Nate took a swig of the cold beer and immediately felt better. The heat plus the drive to Murrieta and back had finally caught up with him. He wanted to head out to Anaheim right away, talk to the orange-haired kid, but no way could he sit in his car for another hour. He'd get some shut-eye first.

Nate caught Clutch up on his case over a pastrami sandwich. When he got to the part about a face-to-face with Ornj, the old man's face darkened.

"I don't want you gettin' mixed up with some Korean gang, son."

"I'm just going to talk to him. Hopefully get something I can give to the police."

"Just give the cops what you have now. Wash your hands of it."

Nate shook his head. "That's just it. I've got shit. Just a possible car sighting and scribbles on a kid's folder."

Clutch sighed. "The least you could do is take Johnny with you."

Nate snorted. "You kidding? That fool never leaves L.A."

On the drive to his apartment, Nate couldn't help thinking the same thing about himself. He grew up in L.A. and would inevitably die in this town. The streets were mean and unforgiving at times, but that was the beauty of it. Los Angeles was like a scorned lover; you never knew if it would show up on your doorstep with a shotgun, or sweet talk its way into your bedroom. He'd take that any day over cookie-cutter homes and mind-numbing planned communities.

Nate had a restless two hours of sleep, and was already awake when his alarm went off at midnight. He made sure his piece was loaded before heading out to the Pegu in Anaheim.

The Pegu turned out to be a one-story building painted brick red. It shared a parking lot with a tire and brake shop. The lot was half-full with sports cars and tuners. A few Koreans stood outside smoking cigarettes. They eyed Nate suspiciously.

Luckily there was no line, probably because it was a Wednesday. Nate walked up to the bouncer, a huge Korean bald dude who looked like he ate rocks and chainsaws for breakfast. He glanced at Nate.

"You ain't comin' in here," he said.

Nate pulled out a wad of cash, peeled off a twenty, placed it in the bouncer's palm. The bouncer stared at it. Nate put down two more. Then two more. The guy nodded and stuffed it in his pants. He jerked his head back.

"I'm looking for Ornj," Nate said.

The guy gazed at Nate with dead eyes. Nate peeled off another two twenties and handed it to him.

"He's in there. Can't miss him."

Nate thanked him and walked into the club. Instantly, he was hit with pulsating electronic dance music and laser lights. The place smelled of sweat, booze, and weed. A Korean DJ was in the booth with headphones on, bobbing his head up and down. A group of girls grooved on the dance floor. Everyone else sat at tables and booths with plates of fruit and bottles. Nobody here was over twenty-five and everyone was Asian. Nate knew he stood out and had to act fast.

He searched the club for bright orange hair, finally spotting the kid in a far back booth, surrounded by four huge Korean dudes. Ornj barely looked twenty-one.

Nate couldn't help noticing the servers who were all male. Every now and then, one would grab a girl from a booth and lead her over to another booth filled with guys. He'd sit her down with them and go do the same thing all over again at a different table. The girl either did a shot with the guys or she'd chat for a bit and then rejoin her friends.

This must be the "booking" Johnny mentioned. Like a weird form of speed dating. But it gave Nate an idea. When one of the servers walked by, Nate pulled him aside. He had to shout to be heard above the pulsing music.

"Do me a favor, man. This hot chick wants to meet Ornj but without his entourage. She's waiting for him in the back room." Nate assumed there were private rooms.

The server narrowed his eyes at him.

"Here." Nate stuffed a handful of twenties in the guy's hand.

The server hesitated, looked down at the money, then nodded. He stuffed the bills in his pocket and gave Nate a thumbs-up.

Nate headed to the back of the club just as a fog machine turned on. The sweet burnt smell of smoke clung to the back of his throat. He walked down a narrow darkened hallway past the bathrooms, a couple young guys giving him the one-shoulder shove.

Nate could find only one private room. The door was shut so he opened it and walked in. A group of well-dressed Korean kids lounging on vinyl booths all turned and looked at him. One guy with glasses stood in front of a small TV screen, a microphone in his hand. A karaoke machine sat on a small table in the corner blasting a K-pop song.

"Hey," one of them said. "We rented this room."

"Not anymore," Nate said. "Everyone out."

Nobody moved. Nate picked up the karaoke machine and threw it on the floor. Plastic pieces flew everywhere. A warped version of the song continued playing until Nate stomped on the machine, silencing it. The kids all leaped up and ran out, wanting nothing to do with the crazy black man. Nate shut the door and killed the lights. He pulled his gun from inside his jacket and waited. After a couple minutes, he heard approaching footsteps.

The door opened and Ornj stepped inside. Nate grabbed him and slammed him against the wall, kicking the door shut. He shoved his gun into the base of the kid's skull.

"What the fuck, man?" Ornj said. He spit the words out as best he could with his face kissing the wall. He thrashed but Nate hung on tight.

"Settle down or I'm blasting a hole in you, you got that?"

"Fuck you," Ornj spat out but he stopped squirming.

"Tell me about Sunny Kim."

"That's what this is about? Shit." His laugh came out as a wheeze. "Just some dumb slut I met out by the casino. Figured I'd work that bitch for some dough."

Nate slammed Ornj's head into the wall again. The kid howled. Nate wanted to rip the motherfucker's head off but he needed information. "But she wouldn't hand over those ducats so you killed her. Is that it?" Nate jabbed the gun harder into Ornj's neck.

Ornj coughed. Blood dripped down his temple into his eyes. "Nah, man. She had jack shit. Was gonna kick her to the curb until she told me about the electronics she could score. Fuckin' primo shit. Got a guy that'd pay top dollar."

"Electronics from where?"

"At the house. That was the last time I saw her, man, I swear."

Ornj's voice rose. "Was waitin' outside for her until it all went to shit. That asshole pulled up with some hot redhead in the car. He ran in so I bounced. Found out the next day she was dead."

"Where?" Nate growled. "What house?"

Ornj told him.

***

By the time Nate arrived in Murrieta, it was close to four a.m. It was still dark out and he breathed in the cool crisp air while he could. The stars shined brighter out here. Maybe because there was no smog.

Nate stopped in front of the Reynolds home and grabbed his gun before walking up to the front door and ringing the bell. After a few minutes of nothing, Nate pounded on the door. A light flickered on and he heard movement inside. The door swung open, revealing a sleepy-eyed Larry Reynolds, wearing boxers and a T-shirt. When he realized it was Nate, he scowled.

"Do you know what the fuck time it is?"

"It's three fifty-eight. Can I come in?"

"No, you can't come in. We're sleeping."

"Looks like you're awake to me. Let me in, Larry. I think you'll want to hear this."

Larry sighed but stepped back, opening the door. Nate walked inside. Margie hovered on the top stairs, a robe wrapped around her.

"What's going on?" she asked.

"Sorry to disturb you, Mrs. Reynolds," Nate said. "I just want to talk to your husband here about Sunny."

"What about Sunny? Did you find out who killed her?" Margie walked slowly down the stairs.

Nate glanced at Larry, who stared at him with cold eyes. "I think your husband may know."

"What? What do you mean?" She stopped halfway on the staircase. "Honey, what's he talking about?"

"I've got no fucking idea," Larry said. His voice was flat.

"What time did you come home from work that day, Mr. Reynolds?"

"I told you. Late. I went straight to bed."

114

"You sure about that?"

"What the hell are you getting at?"

"I have an eyewitness who says he saw you come home around five in the afternoon. He was right across the street. Said a woman waited in your car while you went inside." Nate glanced up at Margie. "A redhead."

Larry went very still. Margie gasped as she clutched the staircase railing. Her eyes narrowed.

Nate continued. "You caught Sunny stealing from you, didn't you, Mr. Reynolds? Had a bag filled with your laptop, video camera, Xbox. Synatech manufactures the most expensive electronics out there. Big demand for them on the black market."

Larry chuckled. "You don't know what the hell you're talking about."

"So you smacked her. Hard. Enough to break her jaw. That dirty little chink. Or maybe you hit her after she took off running. She falls, strikes her head on the pavement."

"You be careful what you're saying, Mr. Hollis. You be very careful." Larry's face reddened and he looked like he was going to come at Nate any second.

"It was an accident, and hey, maybe if you fessed up right away, you'd get away with involuntary manslaughter. Spend a few months in jail. Out early for good behavior."

It was dead quiet in the house, except for the fridge humming in the kitchen.

"But that's not what you did. You calculated, planned. Probably took the girlfriend home first. Made some excuse about the wife coming home early. Then you dumped Sunny's body by the school in the middle of the night and pointed the finger at the Chinese kids." Nate went for a bluff. "I got a witness who can ID your SUV by the field. And I bet if the cops search your car, they'll be able to match the fibers to Sunny's clothes. The rocks in her shoes will match those in your drought-tolerant backyard."

The bluff worked. Larry tackled Nate to the floor. They crashed onto the entryway, Nate striking his head on the cold tile with a dull thud. Excruciating pain shot down his neck and spine. He grabbed a hold of his gun from inside his jacket just as Larry straddled Nate, launching a right to his face, followed by a second one to the gut. The gun flew out of Nate's hand, skittered across the tile. With his hands now free, Nate let loose a flurry of punches until Larry struck him hard in the temple. Nate's head thudded on the tile once again, momentarily immobilizing him.

The crack of a gunshot froze both of them. Margie stood at the bottom of the staircase, about ten feet away, pointing Nate's gun directly at them.

"You fucking bastard," she said, her voice low and animal-like. "You swore you were done with that cunt." She pulled the trigger.

Margie was a terrible shot. The bullet struck far left and Nate took the opportunity to end the fight with a brutal punch to Larry's jaw. He rolled over with a moan, then lay still.

Nate sat up, resisting the urge to puke all over the tile. He looked at Margie, struggling to focus on her with his blurred vision.

"Call the police," he croaked.

***

Nate walked into the ACE office, the familiar mildew smell hitting him. Through a glass partition, he could see Jo Lee and a Korean man sitting in her office. When she spotted Nate, she smiled and came out to greet him.

"Mr. Hollis, thank you so much for coming." She looked stunning in a simple black pantsuit that fit in all the right places. Her brow furrowed. "You okay?"

Nate touched the bandage on his temple. "I'm fine, Ms. Lee. Takes a lot more to bring me down." Truth was his head still ached and his vision wasn't a hundred percent. Doc said he had a concussion and to take it easy for a while.

She nodded, concern still clouding her face. "Come, he's waiting to meet you."

Nate followed her inside the office. The Korean man stood, blinking expectantly at Nate who towered over him.

"Mr. Kim, this is Nate Hollis."

Mr. Kim bowed. Nate returned the gesture. The man offered his hand and Nate shook it. He said something in Korean and Nate looked to Jo Lee.

"He says he's eternally grateful to you for finding the man who killed his daughter."

Nate nodded. "Tell him I'm sorry for his loss."

Thanks to Margie and Nate's statements to the Murrieta PD, Larry Reynolds was arrested for the death of Sunny Kim. Nate hoped the D.A. would push for murder one, but that was a stretch. The best scenario would be manslaughter and obstruction of justice, but guys like Larry would hire an expensive lawyer and be out in a few years.

"ACE is taking care of Mr. Kim's travel expenses and funeral costs, of course," Jo Lee said as if Nate asked. "We run strict background checks on our host families, but clearly that's not enough. We're looking into other methods."

Nate said nothing. No amount of research or database checks can predict what people will do when they're desperate. He looked at Mr. Kim who sat back down wordlessly, staring straight ahead.

As Nate headed out of ACE's office, he got a call from Johnny.

"Misha sends her thanks. You did good, Hollis."

"You're just happy I got her off your back."

A chuckle. "You got that right."

Nate hung up and eased himself into his Dart. The heat wave had let up and it was a balmy seventy degrees. He drove away from ACE's office, thinking of the father staring vacantly into space. It was an image Nate wouldn't soon forget.

THE CASE OF THE MISSING DENTIST

by
Gary Phillips

Tyra Williams crossed her Liz Claiborne-clad pant legs at the ankles and squeezed the Nerf football hard. She wished this toy for the nervous patient was bigger, the size of a Teddy Bear you'd win at the fair, and she could wrap both arms around that bad rascal until the visit was over.

"How's business?" Dr. Marcusa asked nonchalantly as he examined her teeth with the mouth mirror. His deep-set eyes scanning like a gunslinger walking into an unfamiliar saloon.

Did he see remnants of the shrimp scampi she had last night? Even though she'd brushed vigorously then and this morning, also using mouthwash so as not to offend? She hated having to go to the dentist, even if it was only her semi-annual check-up. But her work required her to interact with all types of people and you had to smile, always be smiling, dammit.

The mirror scraped against one of her back teeth and he hmmm'd.

Shit, maybe there was a speck of caramel left from that Snickers she had last week, daring to challenge the laws of accumulation and knowing she'd have to work that much harder in her next spin class to burn off the sugar and fat. She squeezed the football again, veins prominent on the topside of her hand.

Dr. Marcusa replaced the mirror with one of his hook-headed explorer picks. He paused, then put the pick down to pick up a device that was a red rubber bulb with a bent metal tube and nozzle attached. This contained Xylocaine, which he sprayed in more than one area of her mouth. Williams was grateful that the topical anesthesia numbed sensitive areas. The doctor then got to work in her mouth with the pick, getting at the residue between her teeth where they poked free of her gums.

Just imagining this caused her to make a sound in her throat that you can only make when you can't bring your teeth together. Her lips vibrating in a frequency that came out as gobbledygook, the international language of the dental office sufferer.

"Good, good," the doctor said in his pleasant Nigerian-tinged accent, "you've been using your water pick. Not much build up, just a little," he trailed off, concentrating.

Williams scolded herself not to squirm, squishing the football tighter. The tip of the pick was down there in the split between her teeth, rending and tearing, pulling and plucking in the practiced hands of Dr. Oliver Marcusa. How glad she was for the Xylocaine. There was a dull sensation, but it had an remote quality, as if hearing a baseball thump against a thick wall from the other side. But that didn't stop phantom pain from manifesting itself in her brain and nerve endings as the tug and scrape of the instrument went about its scavenging business.

"Go ahead and rinse, Tyra," the doctor said, looking off into the outer room as the front door opened and closed, the murmur of light traffic briefly invading the suite of offices.

She swished the foamy liquid around as best she could in her partly numb mouth, trying not to drool on the paper bib clipped around her neck. She spat into the bowl, disappointed the rinse was pinkish as it swirled down the drain.

"That's okay, that's fine," he said reassuringly as she leaned back on the reclined chair. "That's why there's check-ups." The door to the outer area was ajar and in came two voices. Williams presumed whoever had come into the office was talking to Marcusa's assistant, Edwina.

"Almost done," he said as he picked up a tool and got back to work, tugging and pulling, scraping and seeking out that gummy slow acting acid that eats teeth and destroys gums. Oh God, she imagined horribly, what would it be like if she had to have dentures? Taking them in and out at night after she slipped on her PJs. She squeezed the football again and closed her eyes, doing what she could to relax. How soon would soon be?

Tug and scrape, tug and scrape...

"Doctor,' said the slightly accented voice of Edwina, "sorry to interrupt, but –"

"Yes, yes," he said, impatient and another emotion shading his usually placid tone. "Excuse me just a second, Tyra."

"No problem," she slurred, the numbness making the side of her mouth droop, her tongue doughy. Marcusa stepped out of the room, not quite closing the door behind him. Williams looked over at the poster on the near wall showing happily drawn, sparkling eyed multicultural people brushing and flossing. On the wall opposite was the classic, enlarged photo of the cat drawing itself up on a limb by its paws and the words "Hang in There" printed below the image.

She closed her eyes, idly wondering what if she did a comedy album, the best of jokes and routines about going to the dentist? Would there be a market for that? Or whatever happened to the Muzak they used to play when they put you on hold calling the dentist or medical doc? How about a collection of that, Music for Masochists. She chuckled, lightly tossing the Nerf ball back and forth between her hands. There was a retort, something loud like a book being banged on a counter. She half rose, expecting angry voices but there was only silence, not even the indistinct murmur of voices or movement beyond the slightly open door.

Several minutes went by and Dr. Marcusa hadn't returned. Sitting up again, Williams called out, "Doctor? Edwina?" No reply. She repeated herself and again got no response. She got off the chair and looked out the doorway and saw no one. She stepped further into the outer confines where there was the assistant's counter that led to the waiting room. The door to that was closed as was the sliding glass window looking out on the front. But it must have been opened earlier Williams concluded, having heard the front door opening and closing. To one side where she stood was a closed door, the doctor's office. Tentatively she knocked.

"Dr. Marcusa, are we going to finish?" She heard nothing and pressed her ear to the thin wood. She grunted and tried the knob, which turned. She opened the door some and announced herself. Again, nothing. She stepped into the compact office and saw he wasn't there. He had his own bathroom in here and the door to it was opened inward. She called in there and going more inside, could see that it was empty in there as well. Walking back out, she noted a small African carving on his desk, several coins leaning against its base.

She soon determined there was no one in the suite. "What the hell?" she said aloud. Williams removed the bib and placed it on the assistant's counter. She retrieved her purse from where it was in the inner room and checked her phone. No texts or messages. Well, there was nothing to be done but leave and figure she'd hear from them soon, that some sort of emergency had come up and demanded they had to light out of the office. But what could that have been? A car accident and the poor bastard's teeth were embedded in his dashboard?

She smiled at that and heading for the door, stopped. There was a hole in the front door, a ragged hole clean through to the outside. She bent slightly to look at it closer. It was more or less round and opening the door, could tell that was the exit as the splinters around the hole were pushed out. Had that been caused by a bullet? A bullet shot from within the office? She was pretty certain the hole hadn't been there when she'd come in earlier. She stepped back in the office, looking down on the industrial carpet for blood, but saw none. Williams checked the concrete landing on the other side, clean of any blood drops too.

Williams twisted her shapely lips, considering what to do. She could just leave, not get involved. But what was the use of having a sometime lover who was a private eye if you couldn't ask him for a favor now and then? Back inside the waiting room, she took out her phone and touched a number among her contacts.

"Nate," she said, when the line was answered, "how busy are you?"

***

Nate Hollis parked his refurbished emerald green '69 Dodge Dart at a meter, paid, then stepped into the ground floor office of Oliver Marcusa, DDS which fronted Rimpau "Hey," he said as Tyra Williams got up from her seat in the waiting room They kissed quickly and she told him what happened. At this point they stood by the hole.

"That's from a bullet all right,' he confirmed, his eye close to the door's surface. He had a notion about the caliber but kept it to himself.

"Don't you carry around a magnifying glass like Sherlock Holmes?" she kidded.

Straightening up, he said, "Maybe I should, along with a sleek lock pick kit, if I knew how to pick a lock. Be all super investigator and what not." He opened the door, noting the trimmed hedges fronting the porch to the office. He wondered if there was a spent bullet in there but closed the door again, saying, "You didn't hear anything except that crash or whatever it was?"

"Yes, but like I said, somebody else was out here. That was the reason he stepped out while he was cleaning my teeth."

Hollis, dressed in pressed chinos, moccasin slippers, and a black polo shirt had the appearance of a suburbanite out scouting potential income property. He looked around. "It is odd. What about their cars?"

"There's a little parking area out back. Right now there's only one car there, a late model Camry. I don't know what Dr. Marcusa or Edwina drives, and it doesn't belong to either of the two patients who came by. I told them they weren't around. I checked after the two had come and gone and it's still there."

"Let's go take a look." They walked around back. Hollis bent down to look inside the vehicle, which was clean and free of dings and dents. There was nothing on the seats to indicate who the car might belong to. He took a picture of the license plate with his phone and asked Williams, "We're behind the examining room. Did you hear car doors or voices when you were in the chair?"

"Nate, you know how I feel about dentists, so I was too into my trying-to-be-calm zone to notice."

"Okay," he smiled. They went back inside. Pointing at the way they'd just come, he asked, "Is this the only door in or out?"

"I didn't notice another one."

"Let's see."

Soon they were in the doctor's office. Williams turned the rod to further open the Venetian blinds. Warm light flooded the room. Hollis regarded the orisha statuette on the desk. He leaned closer, cognizant he didn't want to touch it and leave his prints. He looked at it from more than one angle.

He said, "I'm not an expert, but I think that's supposed to be the Yoruba deity Aje."

"And who is he?"

"A she, and she stands for wealth."

"Yeah?"

Hollis glanced over at her and said, "Hold on a sec." Hollis stepped out of the room and returned with Kleenex in his hand. He stepped around to the other side of the desk and sat down. He tried the drawers which were locked. But with the tissues in his hand, he gripped the middle drawer and after a few forceful tugs, broke it open.

"When you talk to the cops, don't mention this. You can tell them I was here as they'll find out we know each other, just leave out the breaking and entering."

"The cops?"

"When I'm done, you should call them and tell them everything." He looked up from rummaging in the drawer. "Who knows how this will shake out, so you want to be the good citizen here. Only not too damn forthright." He resumed snooping.

"Dragging sweet innocent me down to your larcenous level."

"Ha." He lifted something up from underneath a collection of drug and equipment brochures. He held up an object between his fingers, not bothering to use the tissues.

Williams leaned in. "A horse?"

In Hollis' outstretched palm was a small molded piece of plastic in the likeness of a horse. It was generic in design and red, like something used on a game board. "Does he have kids?"

"He's a bachelor."

"He hit on you?"

"He's always been professional, Mr. Hollis."

Indicating the piece she said, "Maybe he's an uncle. A niece or nephew was here and they lost this and he found it."

Hollis was looking at the back of the horse and showed that to Williams as well. "Is that supposed to be a jewel? It was a raised octagonal shape on the horse's back. He rubbed his thumb over the shape.

"Damned if I know."

Hollis sat back in the swivel chair, bouncing the front of his feet off the floor. "What about his assistant?"

"Edwina, but I don't know her last name. She cocked her head slightly. "She did mention in passing she had a niece, so could be she was were here and left the toy."

"Possibly." He pocketed the horse and dug out a letter addressed to the doctor's home, which was in Culver City. He found no personnel file for the assistant. He got up and around from behind the desk. "Let's take a look at her area."

Below Edwina's counter was her purse. In it was her iPhone. Hollis removed it with the tissues and tried to enter its screen but this required a password. He put the phone back. "I know someone who could crack the phone and get me in, 'cause this is starting to look like something shady went down."

Williams touched his arm. "Oh, Nate, you think it was a kidnapping? A double kidnapping?"

"I don't know, Tyra, but it's been what, damn near an hour and a half since this started?"

"Shit," she said a foreboding chill circulating through her.

He put a hand around her waist. "Look, one step at a time, okay? Stay calm 'cause now you've got to do the hardest part."

"Yeah," she said. "But they're going to ask me why I took so long to call them."

"Put that on me. You waited for me to get here and then I looked around. You stayed up front in the waiting room while I prowled around in the back. Understand?"

"Yes," she drew out. "But I want you here when I call them before you bounce."

"Of course. And if they do suddenly get friendly, talking about coming on down to the station to clear this up, you say—?"

"No thank you, and ask am I under arrest?"

Squatting, Hollis was going through the trashcan under the counter. "There you go." He found a receipt from a Stop and Go, scanned it quickly, and pocketed that too. He straightened up. "This Edwina a vegetarian?"

"I don't know," she shrugged. "But sister girl is fit. If I was into the bi thing, I'd make a play for her." She winked at Hollis who smiled.

"Ready?" he asked after a moment.

Williams took out her phone from the back pocket of her pedal pushers. She drew in several deep breaths then made the call to Southwest Division on her mobile. "Hello, yes, I'm not sure if this is anything, but I'm at my dentist's office and he and his assistant are gone, they left as he was working on my teeth." It went on from there until she said, "Right, I'll be here." She disconnected. "They're sending a patrol car."

He gave her a peck on the cheek. She swayed some from nervousness. "Just tell it like we agreed. They'll put their cop stare on you, but you're the one being upright, got it? Like being on the witness stand, say only the facts, don't offer your opinion unless they ask you. And even then, clipped, short answers. Don't be friendly, be like when you negotiate a contract with one of those pants saggin', chronic smokin' big gold cross on the chest 'cause it's all due to Jesus and my mama rappers." Williams ran an indie record label that offered an eclectic roster of talent, from hip hop to old school be-bop.

She said, "They're going to ask me why you didn't stick around."

"Tell them I had to get back to a current matter. Lay my number on them."

"Got it, tough guy."

Hollis gladly noted the nervousness was gone from her voice She had her mind on what lay ahead. He gave Williams' upper arm a reassuring squeeze and left the office. Driving away, he punched in a number on his hands free unit and the line eventually connected after going through various routers and what all else. Hollis didn't get it all, but the man he was looking for did.

"This you, Nate?" a wary voice answered, seeing a certain encryption of numbers and letters that popped up on his screen.

"Yeah, Frag, it's me. You at the spot?" He heard someone shout, "Foul, fool," and rough laughter in its wake in the background. He had a good idea where Frag Lawson was at this time of day, this day of the week. For a man into various conspiracy theories, he was a creature of habit Hollis reflected, and not for the first time.

"Come on, then," and the line was severed.

Hollis drove on, the traffic normal for this time of the morning. He got over to the Hollywood rec center at Santa Monica Boulevard and Cahuenga in less than half an hour. Parking was another matter, but after circling the long block once, a VW pulled away from the curb and he was able to fit in the slot. He walked back to the basketball court where Cyrus "Frag" Lawson was playing.

He was a stocky, thick-fingered cyber geek, who nonetheless had moves on the court. As Hollis stood on the sidelines with some others looking on, Lawson stole the ball from a would be NBAer in neon orange Nikes who'd been trying to be fancy with a crossover move. He drove forward, stopped, spun to avoid an oncoming opponent, jumped, his arms bent textbook perfect at the elbows, and his three-pointer swished in—though there was no net. The hoop had the remnants of the chain links that had formed the so-called netting, but were now a few anemic links hanging off the rim. He played another five minutes or so, then had one of the onlookers sub in for him.

"What up?" Lawson said. He grabbed a towel lying on his gym bag and attacked his sweat. He was in cargo shorts and ragged tennis shoes. Displayed on his t-shirt in jagged letters was Snowden for Communications Czar.

"Looking good, son." They bumped fists.

"Flattery will get you everywhere. What you need, brah?" Lawson was in his early thirties, a lighter shade of black man than Hollis, with medium-length dreads and a goatee that needed tending.

Hollis showed him the receipt. "I'd like whatever info you can call up on the health nut whose credit bought this stuff." On the slip of paper was an asterisk and the last four digits of a credit card used to purchase a bottled kale smoothie and a boxed green salad.

Lawson took the receipt and removed his laptop from the depths of his stuffed gym bag. They sat side by side on the dingy aluminum bleachers as the machine powered up. There was WiFi at the rec center, but Hollis knew that the ever cautious Lawson had rigged his machine to roam for signals elsewhere as he was paranoid about being back-traced. He frequented those conventions where the notion that 9/11 was an inside job was taken for granted. But the odd thing was Hollis knew he'd done back door work for NSA-type shadowy departments of the government. Maybe he did know something the rest of us didn't, he allowed. They were sitting on the top row of the bleachers and below them a blonde woman with spiky hair and torn jeans was hunched over, head between her legs – an addict in the grip of her daily come down, summing the energy to work her hustle to score and start the cycle all over again, Hollis surmised.

Lawson tapped keys and studied his screen as firewalled portals gave way to his cyber hacking skills. "I'm in," he announced. "Would you hold the receipt open for me?"

Hollis held it between both sets of fingers for Lawson to get the numbers off the paper. Much like when you used your credit card in the store and not too much later you'd get an email for a diaper coupon because you'd bought baby food, he was posing as one such vendor of the chain store. Essentially piggybacking his way into their databanks while not leaving a trail, Hollis knew from previous interactions with the techie.

"Edwina Fonseca," Lawson announced. "Got several pages of stuff. I'll send it to your phone."

"Right on." This time Hollis shook his hand as Lawson closed out various screens on his laptop. "As always."

"As always."

Hollis departed and Lawson now stood on the sidelines, eager to go back in after putting his machine away. They used the barter system and he'd return the favor by fulfilling a future request from Lawson. One time he'd asked him to track down a lead to a supposed diary that proved that Martin Luther King, Jr.'s death had been faked by a makeup artist and documentary filmmaker. Naturally no such diary was found, though Hollis did do the rundown, including meeting with a bunch of UFOers outside Taos. Back in reality, based on the information Lawson had unearthed about Edwina Fonseca, including the make and year of her car—which was the Camry at the office—and her current address. Hollis drove to her abode. This proved to be an older apartment building on Saturn in the Mid-City area.

Parking again and walking back to the apartment building, he saw you had to be buzzed into the security-gated complex. To better blend in, he'd put on one of several pieces of clothing he kept in his trunk. With a hard hat tucked under his arm, striped day-glo vest on, and coveralls with Department of Water and Power markings, he looked like that kind of employee. He also had a clipboard and pretended to be making notes, waiting until somebody came out and he'd go in behind them.

A fancy old timey car pulled up, double parking. Off white and whale blue trim. Was it a Rolls circa 1950s? Hollis wondered. The driver, taller than Hollis and wide in the chest, got out and came around to the other side to the rear. The power window slid down and Hollis noted a woman in shadow in there, large dark glasses further obscuring her face. She exchanged words with the dark suited driver and he went up to the security gate, digging keys out of his pocket. He unlocked the gate and went inside. Hollis casually walked in behind him before the gate closed.

The complex was a two-story structure in a kind of squared off U-shape around a concrete and grass plaza. There was a small fenced-in pool off to one side of the area, the entry to which was gained up a set of low steps. The driver went up the outside set of stairs to the second floor and along the walkway. Judging by the procession of numbers on the doors on the first floor, Hollis was pretty certain he was heading toward the apartment of Edwina Fonsesca. Things were definitely getting interesting. He briefly consider bracing the driver, but as he was unarmed, and who knew if the other man was strapped or some kind of kung fu expert, he chose a second approach. He left the premises ahead of the other man and walking away, passed behind the old car. He glanced at the license plate and committed the letters and numbers to memory. Muffled from inside the idling vehicle, he detected...an obo was it? Classical music for sure he concluded. He texted the license plate identification to Frag Lawson after he'd taken off his rudimentary disguise and was sitting in his Dart.

The car turned out not to be a Rolls Royce as he'd guessed, but a 1956 MG Saloon. It was leased to an enterprise called Red Oak Holdings based out of the San Gabriel Valley. About two hours later, Hollis drove out to its offices in Monterey Park, otherwise known as the Southland's Chinese Beverly Hills – or at least one of them. The main drags of the city were wide avenues bifurcated by plant rich median strips where the sidewalks led to banks, hardware stories, trendy and retro clothing stores, and restaurants. These last two types of businesses attracted people from well beyond the immediate community. Hollis was a fan of an eatery here called the Seafood Lake and had been there several times, including dates with Tyra Williams. They'd enjoyed savory repasts of hollowed-out jalapeño peppers stir-fried with salty crumbles of pork; another time an omelet stuffed with shreds of preserved turnip, Chiu Chow-style duck, and simmered in a thick gravy with dried tofu in the mix. He was particularly fond of the oysters with ginger and scallions.

The location of Red Oak Holdings was a lone, plain, low-slung building. It was at the end of a residential street near where the city bordered Alhambra. It was unmarked save for the address in small metal numerals painted in enamel black. This was above a closed wooden door inset with a window, diamond patterns of chicken wire embedded in the glass. On each side of the door were glass bricks and the window in the door had a closed curtain behind it. He tried the knob, which didn't turn, and knocked on the door. There was no response and he didn't hear anything when he pressed his ear to the panel. He didn't see the classic MG sedan in front so he headed toward the rear of the structure. It was then he heard a noise and, stepping back from the corner of the building, a door opened about mid-way down the side of the structure. An older Latino man in baggy pants and a buttoned down shirt clasped at his wrists propped the door open. Hollis almost revealed himself but reconsidered. The man wheeled out a hand truck with several cardboard boxes stacked inside each other and a good-sized trash bag on top of all that. He pushed the trash toward the back and went around the corner. Hollis snuck forward and chanced a look inside. He didn't see anyone else and he quickly went in.

The interior was filled with vending machines of varying sizes and shapes, some of them oval, futuristic in style. Hollis also noted several older models grouped together in an area of the warehouse like museum pieces. Some of the vending machines were bracketed by molded Styrofoam, in turn held to the machines by wide swathes of plastic wrapping. Others were in open boxes and a few were in the stages of being crated up. Looking closer at a particular set of the snack dispensers, Hollis noted these had the Stop and Go logo on them. Emblazoned across the front were the words "Healthy Alternatives." There were no food items in any of the machines, but a frowning Hollis wondered if Ms. Fonseca had bought her kale smoothie from such a machine. And if so, was that the reason her and the dentist had gone missing?

There was also a work area and three machines in states of repair. The older gent seemed to be the only one around, but a toilet flushing disabused Hollis of that idea. Hollis scurried and hid behind the older, taller vending machines off to one side as a door opened and another man, a younger, brown-haired Asian in skinny jeans, stepped out of a bathroom somewhere from the recesses of the shop. The older man who'd been outside came back in then, his dolly now empty of its trash.

"I'm going to finish the two for Pluto Praxis," the older man said to the younger one. From where he was hunkered down, Hollis chanced to peek around the frame of a machine and look at the two as they stood near the work area.

"And I'll get that recalibrating done."

"Okay, good."

The younger one stepped out of Hollis' line of vision and the older one sat and turned up a radio the private eye hadn't realized was on. The volume was still low, but he made out enough to hear it was tuned to one of the oldies stations.

He remained where he was for more than two hours. At one point the younger man left, leaving only the older one who was involved in his work. From the angle he was at, Hollis saw the man's back, his shoulder rolling and shifting under the material of his shirt as he performed circuitry surgery. Wisps of vapor rose from where he sat, where Hollis presumed he was soldering, when his smartphone chimed. He answered, taking off his headpiece with the light magnifying lenses he could swing in and out of place.

Yes, right, I was finishing the one to be delivered to Pluto Praxis." He listened then said, "Okay, I'll get over there right now." He severed the call and got off his stool. He, too, took a trip to the restroom and after that, quit the place. Hollis waited a minute then stepped out. He was heading toward the side door when an idea occurred to him. There was something about this place, these men and their new tech devices he found…curious. Who was that women in the town car, and why had she had her driver rummaging through Edwina Fonseca's apartment? It's not like he returned with an overnight bag for her. He took some pictures of the circuit boards and what have you on the worktable.

After that, at the side door, his hand was extended toward the knob and damned if the door didn't open outward and the younger man stood there.

"Shit."

"Who the fuck are you?" he said, gaping at the stranger.

Hollis grabbed the slimmer man's arm and pulled him inside,

swinging his body around and letting go. The other man stumbled backward, but didn't fall over as Hollis intended. He reached into his back pocket and removed a small canister of pepper spray. He rushed at Hollis, the irritant hissing at the detective's upraised hands and face.

Rather than move backward and thereby receive the full blast, and Hollis knew first-hand what the chemicals did to you, he also surged forward, turning his body sideway like a wrestler about to body slam an opponent. He had an arm up and knocked the can away, though part of the spray caught him in the side of his face, making his right eye water and burn. But Hollis forced pain and panic aside and pressed on. He had to, he couldn't be caught to be hauled away by the cops. Though he had the impression the lady in the swank car wouldn't be eager to have her activities known by the law—all the more reason he had to be victorious.

The young man had good reflexes and had let up on the canister's valve when Hollis had knocked it aside. Now he swung the canister back toward the detective, releasing the orange cloud of pain as he brought it across his body. Hollis put his head down like the tackles that used to bull at him when he was a running back in high school football. He got his arms around the other man's lower legs, the pepper spray wetting the back of his head, his eyes closed to avoid the heated spill. They went over. Hollis drove his elbow into the other's stomach, knocking the wind out of him. The twentysomething's fingers twitched loose on the can. Hollis took it and emptied the remaining contents in the other man's face.

"Motherfucker, motherfucker," he wailed, rolling around.

Hollis sprinted away. His right eye swollen and tearing fitfully, he nonetheless could see fine out of his left. Once behind the wheel of the Dodge, he put some distance between him and Red Oak Holdings. After a mile away, he pulled the car over. Wiping at his eye with the heel of his palm and sniffing loudly, he sent the pictures of the electronics to Frag Lawson with a note. He then resumed driving back into Los Angeles. His next stop was the library, the Washington Irving branch on Washington which was a block or so east of Crenshaw. It wasn't large but had been modernized several years ago, the façade in tones of light beige stone befitting a rest stop of knowledge. Inside it was quiet, the staff responsive, a place for contemplation among the regulars. These included the homeless and under-employed who used the computers to surf the web, the mutterers in search of that one arcane text linking all their theories of the Illuminati and the Nazi lizard race residing underneath the earth, and the merely bored looking for an air-conditioned hideaway who didn't want to drink too early in the afternoon.

Hollis wasn't opposed to research on the 'net, and in fact subscribed to more than one data mining account used by investigators and lawyers. Yet, even though he was only in his thirties, he appreciated the old method of hunting down a particular book, the musty smell of them in the stacks, feeling its heft in your hands and sitting at a desk, absorbing its contents. He was doing that now, two other books on the small table next to him. The third one, about symbols, was open as he read a specific passage. He closed the book and put the tome, a second edition published in the 1940s, atop the other two.

Walking out, he passed by the information desk and the middle-aged black woman sitting there. She had short, grey straight hair, and her eyes moved back and forth behind her stylish glasses as she read a magazine article. She looked up.

"Thanks for the lead about the horse," he said. "You were right on the money."

"Glad it worked out."

Once back in the compact parking lot on the east side of the library, Hollis made a call to Williams. "How'd it go with the cops?" he asked after she answered.

"You owe me dinner and drinks, you bastard," she said wearily. "And I don't mean one of them hole in the wall joints you're forever dragging me to."

He suppressed a smile, knowing a person with a practiced ear like hers would know he was grinning. "Sorry, babe, I'll make it up to you. They didn't believe you?"

"Aw who the hell knows what them po-pos believe. All I know is they played hot and cold with me. I guess at first I was just some chick on her monthlies getting her soap operas mixed up with reality. But the hole in the door got their attention and they started playing a different hot and cold with me, hinting about 'Why don't I come on down to the station and have a cup of coffee so they make sure they get this right.' Like maybe I took a shot at the doc, asking me had we dated. Sheet, I didn't just get here on the turnip truck. But I knew to hold back. So once I gave them you, they switched gears."

"Yeah?"

"Yeah, the lead one made a call out of earshot and he came back and conferred with the other one. They let me go on my merry way soon after that."

Hollis heard a ping, announcing a new text message had come in on his phone. He continued talking to Williams. "They look for the slug?"

"Not with me there, no."

"You did good."

"Damn right I did. Find out anything?"

"Not sure yet. But I think the horse is a good luck symbol, a zen sort of thing. The jewel on its back is double luck, I'm figuring. Is the doc superstitious?"

There was a pause on the other end as she reviewed her past visits to the dentist. "Last year when the Comets made it to the playoffs, we were chatting about one of the upcoming games. He was standing by his cabinet and opened it twice quickly, shutting it quickly too, tapping his foot and saying something like 'Here's hoping they do,' or something like that."

"You do that, Nate," she said, her tone softening. "Call me later."

"I will." He clicked off and read the text message. It was from his grandfather Obadiah "Clutch" Hollis, a pioneer pro football player in Los Angeles with the Rams and the short-lived Marauders in the '60s The old man was still vital, and ran a friendly bar and grill in the Crenshaw District.

"A plainclothes dropped by to see you. Said I'd give you his message."

"Thanks," he texted back. "I'm coming over." He took the LAPD detective dropping around to mean they'd found the slug. But he didn't think they were so anxious to get to him that the cop would be staking out the Hideaway, the establishment his granddad co-owned. Or at least he was going to find out if the place was being watched. Soon he arrived there.

"Number one grandson," Clutch Hollis said when the younger

Hollis knocked briefly, then stepped into his small back office in the bar. The elder Hollis was dressed in khakis and a worn work shirt. He was at his desk going over invoices and other such paperwork. Several boxes of supplies like cocktail napkins with the bar's logo on them were stacked near him.

"When was this?" the private eye said, stepping more into the room, pointing at a new photo on the wall behind and to the side of the desk. Inside the drugstore bought frame, a smiling Clutch Hollis was standing and shaking the hand of the smiling head coach of the Rams football team, the young bike riding Sean McVay. Both were turned toward the camera, and Hollis was pretty certain the shot had been taken on the field at the Coliseum. It was their past and now temporary home stadium, which was not far away in South L.A. The team had returned to their adopted hometown after leaving for St. Louis at the close of the 1994 season. A new stadium where they—and now the Chargers, who moved from San Diego down south—would be residing in was being built in Inglewood, a nearby municipality.

"Aw, they had some of us old timers still upright and not too delusional yet come down and meet and greet. You know, like a pastor gives his benediction." He chuckled at that. "And what the hell, a few players might drop by for a beer and a sandwich, and that wouldn't be a bad thing."

The younger Hollis said, "You still got a few friends who're all up in the black frat scene?"

The older man sat back, tapping his pen against his other hand. "What you working on, Mannix?"

He told him what had happened up to now.

His grandfather said, "And this missing dentist is in a fraternity?"

"I didn't see anything in his office indicating that, but a lot of professional brothers of a certain age are, so wanted to check."

Clutch Hollis stared off then focused back at his only grandson. "Maybe whatshisname," he tapped the blunt end of the pen on the desktop, "He's had me at his box for a few Comets' games. Damn, his name is, Mark….Mark Dansker, might be the one to talk to."

"Dansker?" his grandson said, eyebrow raised.

His grandfather grinned. "Got some German somewhere in the family but he's dark enough. He was on the Kappa's national board at one point, I seem to recall."

"The Divine Nine, isn't that it?" Nate Hollis observed about the collection of the historic black fraternities and sororities.

His grandfather shrugged. "The Alpha Phi Alphas and what have you."

"Who is he?"

"A lawyer by training. Not as flashy as Johnnie Cochrane, but in his time he put in the work, helping overturn the restrictive housing covenants here, school busing issues and was also big in the NAACP chapter in town." He looked down at his desk, frowning. "Somewhere around here I must have a number for him. He's been more or less retired, but still does consulting at his old law office."

"You remember the name? I can look it up on them internets."

"No, don't run off, let me rummage."

"I'll be in front." Along the short hallway from the office, he stopped at the swing door leading to the small kitchen where Trinity Ortiz did chef duty daily from 11 to 5. He was a tatted 24-year-old who had a cosplaying girlfriend and was attending grad school in urban planning.

"Trini, could I get a party melt and some of those zucchini rings of yours?"

"Heavy on the grilled onions, Nate?" The kitchen was decked out in stainless steel and gleamed like a combat jet's newly shined hull.

"If you please."

Not too much later, Hollis was halfway through his meal when his grandfather joined him in the front. He sat next to him at the bar.

"Talked to Mark and he's going to make a few calls. He thinks this dentist of yours sounds familiar. I gave him your cell number." He put a card down on the bar. In addition to the print was a silver and gold shield in relief. "That detective left his card for you." The name on it was Colson Dawes. Hollis knew a few members of the department, but not this man.

He nodded at the card, swallowing. "Great, thanks, Clutch." He finished, paid, though as usual he hadn't been given a bill, and said his good byes. That evening Hollis brought Pan Asian-Cuban fusion takeout over to Tyra Williams' apartment in the area between West Hollywood and Beverly Hills, after they'd talked on the phone.

"Hey," she said after she opened the door. She was dressed in jeans and a loose top that was off the shoulder on one side. She had slippers on her feet. She gave him a kiss and let it linger.

"Hey yourself," when their mouths separated.

They ate on the couch on paper plates at her coffee table. The apartment was decorated in comforting tones of lavenders, browns, and burnt orange. She routinely changed the furnishings and color schemes.

"You hear back from the cops?"

"A detective called me."

"Dawes?"

"Yes. Said he's coming by the office tomorrow. You still ducking them?"

"Not exactly. But his looking around means neither of the two has turned up yet."

"You think it's bad, Nate?" Concern in her voice.

"I think," he began to say, but his phone chimed. He picked it up off the table, not recognizing the number on the screen. He made a face at Williams and answered the call. "Hello?"

"Is this the young Hollis who is related to that rascal Obadiah?"

"Yes sir, is this Mr. Dansker?"

"Indeed, good sir, indeed."

Hollis heard ice tinkling in a glass on the other end. The old gent was probably in his argyle socks enjoying his nightcap. He looked at an inquisitive Williams as he talked. "Do you know Dr. Marcusa?"

"I know of him. He's not in our Greek, but we have a few mutual friends and we've hobnobbed a bit over time."

Hollis explained why he'd called about the dentist. "Is he a gambler?" he asked.

There was a gulp as the other man had more of his drink. "We've played poker in the past."

"Is it your impression he had more than a recreational interest in the sporting life?"

"Didn't realize I was being deposed, young Hollis." There was mirth in his voice.

"I like to be thorough, Mr. Dansker."

"Very good. Not to speak out of turn, but in the interests of your goal of making the unknown, known, I do understand Oliver pursued certain avenues when it came to elevating the stakes."

Though he was doing the lawyer thing of offering back only what he'd been asked, a hint of more lurked behind his words.

"Do you mean extra-ordinary sort of games of chance? Possibly you accompanied him on one of these excursions?" The image of the woman in her bug-eyed sunglasses sprang into his mind. "Maybe involving a password or token to gain entry? A horse with a jewel on the back, symbolizing wealth or good luck?"

Another sip on the other end. "I see you are not a hobbyist when it comes to the art of detection."

"As I said, Mr. Dansker, I like to be thorough."

"Let me make a couple of inquiries. I wouldn't like anything to happen to brother Marcusa or that wonderfully delightful assistant of his. I'll be back in touch."

"Looking forward to hearing from you." Hollis tapped the phone icon to sever the call and put the thing aside. Down at the base of his spine, a bio-electrical current hummed. It wasn't coursing through his body yet, but it would.

"You have that look on your face," Williams said, hand on his knee.

"I like to believe I'm more inscrutable."

She moved her hand more along his inner thigh. "I read you like the front page of the newspaper, Mr. Hollis."

They kissed and tongued and moaned, Hollis cupping her breast with his hand and rubbing his thumb over her stiffening nipple. At first gently, then urgently, they took each other's clothes off. They made love there in the living room, on the sofa and the floor, only getting into bed later to sleep. Early in the morning, Williams kicked him out.

"Now don't pout," she'd said, making a kissy face, "but I have to drive out to Irvine to meet with this act. They're in college there and can only do this before their classes."

Hollis stretched and made bear sounds in his throat. "I got time to make coffee?"

She leaned over onto him, her breasts squashed against his chest. "I need you to leave, Nate, so I got my mind on my money

138

and my money on my mind, boo." As she said this she stroked him, but stopped as he began to automatically respond. "Otherwise I might have to give you some head, and how would that look? Me going around with a drop of your man juice on the side of my plump, red lips." She smiled to make an octogenarian think he was fifty, and kissed his chest.

"You're cold as Trekker at a My Little Pony convention, baby. You missed your calling as a torturer for Trump at Gitmo."

"Um-hmmmm." She got out of bed and sauntered into her bathroom, Hollis staring at her marvelous backside in a thong.

A reluctant Hollis got back to his Fairfax District duplex to shower and shave. Hungry, he drove the short distance east to CJ's on Pico Boulevard. This was the original location of the eatery that combined Mexican and quasi soul food. "From the South to South of the Border" went the saying on their website. There were still corner liquor stories and body and auto repair shops on this stretch of Pico as this was part of the Tenth District, a once heavily black working to middle class neighborhood. It was a place from where Tom Bradley, policeman, attorney, councilman, and mayor, had launched his political career back in the early '60s.

Nowadays off the boulevard, there were homes going for more than a million dollars, where the hipsters and flippers were tearing down the historic Spanish-Mediterranean models and replacing them with three story spare, linear box-like structures more suited for houses made for a lunar sub-division.

At CJ's the mix was blue collar city workers like garbage men and longtime residents who canvassed for Bradley, L.A.'s first black mayor. Second if you counted the Latino and part black Pio Pico who gave the streets his name from the 1800s. There were also twenty and thirty some odds who worked from home or worked in one of the many attendant enterprises servicing The Industry, the movie and TV business, and a famished private eye. Hollis had been denied torrid wake up sex, but was still in need of satisfying at least a modicum of his gluttonous desires.

Hollis was on his second cup of coffee, forking down his breakfast of fried catfish, grits, and scrambled eggs when his phone chimed. He swallowed and wiped his mouth with his paper napkin and beeped his phone on.

"Good morning, seeker of sanity."

Mr. Dasker?"

"It is I. Are you engaged in anything tonight you can't get out of?"

"I'm around."

"I'm glad to hear it."

Hollis sensed the man's smile through the phone.

***

Glenrock House was a 25,000-square-foot Beaux Arts construct impressive even by San Marino standards, a nearby ritzy municipality known for its parachute children. They were the sons and daughters of well-off Chinese nationals who bought houses to park their spoiled, high school offspring under the titular guidance of a caregiver or maybe a host family or relative. In an incident that captured the jaded attention of media over-dosed Southlanders, three of the kids sent there, a male and two females, kidnapped another young woman. The parachuters took her to a local park, slapped her around, stripped her naked, punched and kicked and burned lit cigarettes on her. The motive revealed in court was that the leader of the assault had felt the 18-year-old girl, had disrespected her in some way, then had the temerity to cheap out on her part of a restaurant bill. It had been dubbed a modern day *Lord of the Flies*.

Arriving at the parking area for Glenrock House, the incident and the history he'd learned of the house ran through his mind. From what the somewhat retired lawyer Dansker had told him, the owner, a Mrs. Kalish, had also bought the modest mansion below her and torn it down to build a two-story garage for her vintage car collection and parking structure – where he was now.

"Very good, sir," said the valet when Hollis stepped from his Dodge and handed over the keys. He was a close shaven head Chicano who cast an appreciative eye on the car.

"GTS with the 440 big block," Hollis told him, referring to the size of the engine under the hood.

"That's what I'm talking about, home," he answered, offering his fist.

Hollis gave him a bump and joined a few others making their way up the hill. There were steps and a motorized mini-tram. Men wore suits or jeans and sport coats. The women were in fashionable but casual after hours attire, ranging from dresses to slacks and jeans as well, with a few decked out androgynously in men's bulkier clothes. He took the stairs and was proud he was only slightly winded when he reached the top. He sucked in air and regarded the massive manse. He estimated it took a staff of ten people or so to keep such a place maintained. You finished polishing an end table on one side of the monstrosity, it was time to hike back to the other end and start all over again.

"Welcome," a man in a tan suit and gold tie said at the door. His eyes were shaded by blue tinted lenses in black frame glasses. "You are here to enjoy your whims."

Mr. Dasker had been of the opinion that by coming to this once in a while soiree of Mrs. Kalish, leads to the disappearance of the doctor and Ms. Fonseca might be forthcoming. Hollis had thanked him, inwardly noting he'd never told him the woman was missing too. But you had to go where the case took you, even right into a trap. He was of the opinion that it was Mrs. Kalish in that MG Saloon. It was an old-fashioned vehicle, and while he didn't get a chance to look in her garage, he bet it was sitting in there.

Inside the cavernous rotunda of a foyer, the vaulted ceiling had been painted in the style of the Italian Renaissance, with winged zaftig female angles draped in billowing strips of cloth. The hung blown-glass chandeliers and the windows were draped with Fortuny curtains. He fetched a drink from a passing waiter and wandered into what was probably called the ballroom. Inside was a mini casino. Two roulette wheels were spinning, the distinctive sound of the marble bouncing over the painted hardwood the clack-clack of win and loss to the participants. There were also tables where faro, poker, and blackjack were being played. Hollis hung around watching. At one point a well-dressed older black man with a cane nodded briefly at him. Was this Dansker? He didn't bother the gentleman as he doubled down on his 18 at the blackjack. Hollis stepped out onto a balcony. As it would turn out, he would be playing for different kinds of stakes tonight.

The house was built such that part of it was terraced down the hill it resided upon. The view to the immediate north was of the range of the San Gabriel mountains. This was in the nearby Angelus National Forest, a vast federal reserve that offered camping grounds, hiking, fishing, and skiing when there was snow on those mountains. But years of the state's drought, its dire effects mostly felt in the middle to the south of California, meant the snow season was shortened or often non-existent when it had been regular in years past.

"Do you enjoy the outdoors?" A woman who'd come up quiet as smoke next to him asked. She was ash blonde and had the shoulders of a long distance swimmer. Her eyes matched the turquoise shimmer of her dress. She smelled of rosewater and sandalwood, noticeable but not overwhelming.

"I like to fish now and then," he said. "But I prefer the city where there's still plenty to discover. How about you?" He didn't register her as the woman he'd clocked in the MG sedan. Though her face had been obscured by her over-sized sunglasses, what he'd seen of her cheekbones and lines around her mouth suggested an older, though handsome, woman.

"I enjoy a number of extra-curricular activities," she said, her tone just a shade above neutral. Enough so that a man, if he wanted, might read more into what was said or sidestep the implication.

"This is a hell of a place, huh?" he said, trying to extend the conversation.

"You're new around here. I'd remember someone like you."

He nodded his head toward the game room. "You much of a gambler?"

"Oh I am, but not for the ordinary." Her eyes flared from within as she sipped her martini. "It's the Arena of Will I particularly enjoy."

There it was, the game within the game that went down at Glenrock, the one his sometimes ally Irma "Deuce" Ducett, bounty hunter had told him about. This was after he'd gotten the call from Dansker and had made a few calls of his own, asking around about the place to gather as much information as he could before coming here tonight.

"Way I heard it, Hollis," she told him over the phone, "and this from a bail bondsman I've done some work for in that neck of the woods, is this Kalish has her hands in a whole lot of illicit pies. Something of a queenpin, if you see what I'm sayin', out there in the San Gabriel Valley. And surprise, surprise, like a lot folks with more money than right, she likes to indulge." Deuce had told him some more, but then had to get off the phone as he'd called her in the middle of a stake out and her quarry was on the move, a bail jumping deacon who'd absconded with funds from a megachurch in Long Beach.

Hollis now followed the lady in the turquoise dress along a carpeted hallway paneled in maple. He wasn't sure, but he bet the paintings hanging on the walls, abstracts to conventional pieces, were originals. Like in one of those old B movies on TCM about the haunted mansion, they came to what appeared to be a dead end. She pressed a hidden stud and the wall swung outward. Down they went and as they descended, motion vibrations rose through his shoes. The air itself was charged Hollis realized, like when you went to a sports stadium to see your team. Adrenaline, pheromones, and all else humans gave off when excited assailed him as they reached the bottom of the steps. They were before three good-sized men in suits, sans ties. They stood or leaned before a set of twelve feet tall maple double doors.

One of the men, and Hollis recognized him as the driver of the MG, acknowledged the woman.

"Good to see you, Ms. Lance."

"Likewise, Perceval."

Perceval turned his head on his bull neck ever so slightly toward Hollis. "Sir." If he recognized him from Edwina Fonseca's apartment, he didn't let on.

But it wasn't as if the private eye didn't have an inkling of what was about to happen. He was as prepared as he could be. Perceval tugged on one of the wrought iron knobs and the doors opened on hydraulic hinges. Hollis stepped through after the woman. Perceval also came inside and the doors whispered closed again.

"Please remove your sports jacket and shirt," the driver-bodyguard said. He had a gun on Hollis.

He did as ordered, setting his clothes on a small metal table. Where they were was austere in its Spartan-like decor, like a boxer's locker room before a bout.

"Thank you," Perceval said as he patted Hollis down.

Ms. Lance regarded Hollis, eyes shining like cut gems.

"This ain't no kind of Mandingo thing going on, is it?"

She touched his abs, letting her fingers linger. "Good luck, Nate Hollis."

The woman opened a door behind her and indicated he step into a pit area. Like the jewel on the back of the horse, the arena was octagonal in shape, lined with dull plated metal walls topped with cyclone fencing. Behind the fencing were men and women in casual dressy attire, most wearing beaded and feathered Mardi Gras masks. The door closed. As Deuce had warned him, this was the main event at Glenrock House, at least when it was gambling night.

There was a break in the fencing where a podium resided. It was matte black trimmed in wide bands of gold. Onto this stepped the man in the tan suit. He didn't wear a mask.

"Sports fans, once again we have two challengers who will compete for your bloodlust enjoyment in the Arena of Will. The contest of all contests, is it not?" He said, raising his arms and raising his voice.

Whooping and hollering went up from the assembled. The skunk smell of marijuana drifted down to Hollis, along with the sound of sloshing ice in glasses. Across from him, another door opened and out stepped a woman about Hollis' color, clad in yoga pants and a sports top. More cheers and applause boomed off the walls. His opponent was toned, deft arms and muscular legs. She'd fought here before, Hollis surmised. His stomach tightened and gurgled. It wasn't from fear so much as he had a bad feeling who this was across from him. That, and she looked like she was into this, not being forced to fight as he was. He considered he could tell this bunch he refused to fight, but he figured they wouldn't give a shit and homegirl would still look to take his head off.

There was the soft whine of gears meshing and not far from him came a small metal loop through a slot in the floor, which set itself. Were they going to tether him to that by his ankle? A matching eye ring had risen near the woman across from him. Into the eight-sided arena came Ms. Lance. He held a stout snake in each hand by their respective upper bodies, the rest of them languidly coiling around her forearms. One of the reptiles was interspersed red and yellow with black bands, and the other a black scaly body that gleamed sleek and oily under the overhead fluorescents suspended from the ceiling. She smoldered with an arctic calm.

"So here it is," said the announcer in the tan suit. "The rules are simple. The combatants battle until one can't go on either because of being beaten into submission, maimed or...death." The last word was said unanimously by the masked. "You all," and he swiveled toward the gathered, "will place your bets with our lovely accumulators as always. To add to tonight's festivities, know that each of our contestants has an added incentive to win."

The half-shadowed shapes past the shoulder of the announcer shifted and brought Oliver Marcusa to the front. Hollis knew his face from the dentist's website. He was dressed as he must have been when he was taken from his office. The man showed strain and looked about for succor, but found none among the hungry glares devouring him behind the many pairs of eyeholes.

"Not to go into too much detail," tan suit man was saying, "but suffice it to say Dr. Marcusa strayed from the reservation, seeking to profit from our endeavor. Our private playground of challenge and heartbreak."

"The winner determines his fate, is that it?" Hollis yelled.

The man in the tan suit beamed down at him. "You catch on fast, detective." Chuckles echoed around the arena. For the first time, Hollis saw that to one side of the imprisoned doctor was a woman in a cream-colored dress, her svelte figure accented through the material. Her black hair was swept up high and she fancied over-large false eyelashes and dark eye shadow. Hollis had a hard time placing her ethnicity, but he was sure this was Kalish.

"Place your bets, ladies and gentlemen," the announcer said. Moving through the crowd were scantily clad women with hand held devices to record the bets from the players.

The snake woman snapped open an eye ring and placed one of her creatures down in such a way that when she closed the ring, the snake wriggled and reared its upper body back, but could not slither away. When it opened its jaws, Hollis noted its fangs. Whether those grooved teeth were channels for poison, he didn't know. But just a bite from one of those scaly bastards wouldn't be pleasant.

Hollis and Edwina Fonseca locked gazes. She had on her game face, and it was clear she was in this to win it. Hollis forced himself not to expend mental energy trying to fit the rest of the pieces of the puzzle together. Right now, he too had better get his head on right. She rolled her shoulders, working her head back and forth, eyes lit from within. The snake woman finished securing her pets. Now the ash blonde held silken scarves. A small bell was attached to one end of each scarf. She went to the other woman first and tied it around her eyes. She then came over to Hollis.

"I so want you to win," she oozed to him.

Her words left him cold rather than enticed. Between her and the snakes, her blood was icier than theirs he conjectured. She blindfolded him too. Ms. Lance touched him on the shoulder and he wanted to wretch. "Do well, my darling. Oh, and don't try and remove the blindfold as that would automatically disqualify you. And you wouldn't want to be disqualified." Her subtle scent drifted away from him.

Enveloped in black, Hollis momentarily remained still. He strained to decipher the location of the other bell among the lowered voices rather than stumble about, panicked. To his right, he heard the dinging of the other bell accompanied by a disturbance in the air as Fonseca took a swing at him that didn't connect. He could hear because the bettors had quieted down. They were regulars, and knew the fun was in the blinded participants straining to hear the bell, hoping to locate their antagonist and not be caught unawares of the snakes, who had their fangs poised.

He backed up, moving his arms and hands circularly in case she invaded his space. The problem was as he moved, his bell sounded and could cover her movements. The back of his foot brushed against something and he side-stepped, wary that the snake would latch onto his ankle. Stay focused, he warned himself. Don't fixate on anything else but surviving this crazy fight. Quieting the thudding of his heart in his ears, Hollis detected a spike in the murmuring as if it were a shock to a nerve—they saw what he couldn't see, but he better be ready. He then detected the rush of rubber-soled feet across the concrete floor of the arena. Fonseca collided with him, a tangle of her hands and arms with his. Her fists jabbed and hooked, one of her swings finding his jaw. Hollis sagged but knew he couldn't go down – at least not as she wanted him to do. More punches were thrown, another blow catching him in the middle of his body, but fortunately not knocking the wind out of him. But he pretended he was hurting as he whooshed out a gust of air, doubling over.

"Got you, motherfucker," Fonseca snarled, pummeling him with short, choppy punches, not wanting to draw her fists back too far least he slip away.

But Hollis wanted her close and, like he'd done at the vending machine facility, got his arms around her waist and rose. But this time he didn't intend to tackle his opponent.

"Let go," she railed, hitting him across his shoulders and upper back. He gritted his teeth, sweat stinging him blindly. If he let go, he was done for.

"Ughhh," Hollis grunted, and like a TV wrestler, he reared back, sweeping her body upward then slamming her down onto the desk. He heard a satisfying moan from her, which helped him zero in with a kick to her body. The crowd responded as if they, too, had been struck collectively. Continuing his wrestling moves, he dropped to his knees, hands darting about to grab onto her before she could roll away. In this way, he jabbed her in the rib cage and she groaned again. Yet she wasn't done and she flipped onto her side, scissoring him between her legs.

Fonseca got her hands on Hollis' torso, attempting to pull him closer and get her arms around his neck. Maybe this was how she'd subdued whoever else she'd fought in the eight-sided ring, he projected.

"Godblessit," his grandfather would say when frustrated, trying not to swear and thus offending God and worsening his predicament. The words had spilled out of Hollis' subconscious as her damn fingers seemed to be powered by GPS, probing and grasping him expertly. Her nearness to him meant he had a bead on her too, and his compact left hook glanced off her face. This didn't affect her much, but set her up for his head butt that connected, Hollis having guessed where her face was by her quickened breathing. She grunted loudly and fell back. Hollis crawled like a soldier under enemy fire and found himself partially on top of her, not allowing her to wriggle off. He also counted on her not being fully recovered from his attack. But a sudden hiss deflated his elation.

"Shit," he said. Their thrashing about had brought them nearer to one of the snakes. "I don't know how close we are to your fanged buddy," he told Fonseca, "but do you want to find out if we're in striking range?'

"They're poisonous, you idiot," she said. "We have to be still."

He had an arm over her taut stomach and the forearm of his other arm pressed under her jaw. "Don't forget who has who, Edwina. All I have to do is shove you toward one of 'em."

"Okay, okay," she said, seemingly defeated.

"Tap out," he demanded, shoving his forearm harder under her jaw.

"Yeah," she said calculating he might let off the pressure. He backed off some and Fonseca sat up quick, seeking a hold with both of her hands on his arm so as to twist it out of the socket.

But Hollis had suspected she might have been bluffing, and as she took hold he got to a knee and thudded his upper body into hers. They hit the floor with a fleshy smack, sliding some. There was a gasp from the bettors and a shriek from Fonseca filled the arena.

"Oh, God, oh, God, forgive me," Fonseca implored.

Hollis whipped off his blindfold to see Fonseca running around blindly, the snake latched onto her bicep. She was terrified and hadn't had enough presence of mind to remove her blindfold. The bell dinged out a rhythm of deathly fear as she bounced off the walls. Up in the gallery, people began clearing out, including a man with a limp using a cane. The PI stalked over to the woman and taking off his shoe, used the heel to hit the snake in the head until it was dazed and let go. She sat down, trying to tie the blindfold around her wound.

Hollis looked around, sweating and taking in lungfuls of air. The freed snake had slithered off into the shadows and the other one, still trapped in the eye ring, had curled up, looking like it was asleep.

"Don't let me die, please don't let me die," Fonseca cried, still working nervously on her tourniquet, unable to get it tied.

The King snakes used in the octagon were not poisonous, as Edwina Fonseca had been led to believe. They had a hell of a bite, but did not dispense venom. As she recovered in the hospital, Fonseca told her version of the story as did Oliver Marcusa.

"So girlfriend got all caught up," Tyra Williams noted later. She and Hollis were at the Hideaway, having a drink in one of the booths.

"Looks that way," he said, hand on his beer, but he didn't take a pull.

From what was pieced together, about half a year ago Marcusa convinced his dental assistant, who worked out seriously and had expressed interest in auditioning for one of those physical challenge shows on TV, Extreme Ninja or some such, to explore the real thing. She competed three times successfully, and each time he'd bet on her. Seems they'd also figured out how to cheat. She would super glue a sliver of a straight razor underneath one of her nails, placed there with his help and use of his dental tools. In this way, she was able to put tiny slits in her blindfolds to see, not well, but an advantage nonetheless. But she got found out and ratted out the doctor, who had designs on making more money than just on the arena bouts. He was writing a tell-all book, figuring Idris Alba or Denzel Washington would play him in the big screen version.

"So it was Perceval who'd come by the office and flashed his gun with a silencer on it," Williams offered. "To make the point that the dentist and her had no choice but to come along. He'd shot through the door."

"Yeah," Hollis agreed "Of course, Kalish always figured she could lawyer up and keep anything from coming to light."

"Until you leaked your footage."

Hollis showed teeth. He'd had Frag Lawson outfit him with a body cam on his belt. Hedging that if he didn't return from Greyrock, maybe the authorities would find the evidence on his abandoned body – assuming a search would be done in the Angelus National Forrest, a not uncommon dumping ground for several bodies over the years – perhaps Kalish having been responsible for her share there as well.

At present, Mrs. Kalish, who was of Portuguese, Madagascar and French origins, was believed to be out of the country. The mansion was closed up and a few of the regular participants had been identified due to the digging of several reporters. The partiers included a sitting judge, a deputy district attorney, and an actor with a cult show on cable – though she claimed she was just there for research.

Williams put the L shapes of her thumb and index fingers together to make a rectangle, lining Hollis up in a head shot.

"When I produce a movie about you, who do you see playing you?"

He didn't miss a beat. "More importantly, who plays the snake charmer?"

She twisted her plum colored lips. "Some white broad with a big rack I imagine."

"Damn, you some kind of mind reader, Tyra?"

She leaned over, showing him her open palm. 'Can you guess what I'm going to do next?"

"Just kiddin,', baby, just kiddin.'

"You better be." .

They kissed. Outside a car rolled up to the Hideaway, paused, and when the occupant in the back seat lightly tapped his cane on the side window, the car continued on. An onlooker might well have mistaken the late '50s MG Saloon for a Rolls Royce.

***

"You know that circuitry you photographed in that place?" Frag Lawson said to Hollis about a week later at the basketball court.

"What about it, swami?"

""I'm not sure without seeing them in person, but I'm pretty certain that's surveillance electronics."

Hollis frowned at him. He'd driven by Red Oak Holdings, and damned if the place wasn't cleared out. He confirmed this because he sat at the place for hours, no sign of life. He then removed his crowbar from the trunk, his all purpose breaking and entering or slapping a recalcitrant fool in the head tool, and broke in the side door. The interior was cleaner than a nun's frock. One day not too long after that, he was driving back from giving a deposition at a Westside law firm on an old case when he pulled into a Stop and Go for a juice. One of the futuristic vending machines he'd seen earlier at Red Oak was in there, dispensing healthy choices for food. He stared at the machine and wondered if it was staring back at him, recording his every move.

REPARATIONS

by
Naomi Hirahara

Nate Hollis was on his last dime when he got a call from a woman he had met in a bar in Chinatown. He had actually spent his second to last dime on her without getting her phone number, but she accepted his. "I'll call you when I need some guy followed," she said, laughing as she finished off her Corona.

Now he was hearing the same voice on his phone the next day. "You said that you were getting into the P.I. game, right?" she said.

"Who's this?" Hollis held his flip phone to his ear as he navigated his car, a vintage emerald green Dodge Dart.

"How soon we forget. Last night. Monica Orozco. Well, I know someone who needs a P.I."

"That was quick."

"What can I say? I'm fast."

"You said it, not me." He tried to keep it light, but he was really liking this woman. He reminded himself to save her number.

"It's a son of a woman who looked after me as a baby. We lived in the same neighborhood in Boyle Heights. A Japanese guy, Richard Yamamoto."

Monica explained that Richard's mother, Michi, had died last year in 2002. "She was in one of those World War II internment camps. I think in Wyoming. Michi never liked to talk about it and told everyone, including Richard, that she wasn't going to accept reparations for what happened. And then he was going through her papers recently and he found out that she actually received the twenty grand from the government. He thinks that maybe the caregiver took it."

"That's messed up," Hollis said.

Monica agreed. "The caregiver is this woman named Yolanda Washington."

"Hold on. She's black? Is that why you called me?" Hollis usually didn't care why someone was hiring him, as long as their checks didn't bounce. But with Monica, he hoped that the interest was more personal than professional. To discover that it may be a race-based hire was hard to take.

"Of course not," Monica said. "The caretaker does happen to be African American, but that's beside the point." Hollis knew she was lying. She was a lawyer for Legal Aid, wasn't she? Hollis had rubbed elbows with enough lawyers while working for City Hall in Los Angeles that he knew how they operated. "Michi was like my second grandma. If someone stole her money, her family's legacy, this needs to be made right. Also, wouldn't this gig help you out on your new career?"

"It's not that I'm desperate," Hollis said, although he really was.

"Well, if you're open to it, I can meet you –"

"Okay." Hollis was hoping she meant at another bar, but he was wrong.

"At the Yamamoto house in Boyle Heights. Five tonight. I can introduce you to Richard."

"He's not your boyfriend, is he?"

"C'mon," Monica said. "He's not my type."

"What is your type?"

"You know," she said and then recited the address for the Yamamotos.

The house was on a quiet street that was just below Whittier Boulevard.

The Yamamoto house had obviously seen better days. While the other neighboring ranch-style homes were well maintained and landscaped, this one had dying grass and peeling paint. Hollis didn't mean to stereotype, but he expected a house owned by Japanese Americans would be neat and tidy.

No one was home and judging from the advertisements and junk mail that was left on the weathered welcome mat, no one came here on a regular basis.

Hollis gave Monica a quick call, but it went straight to a voice message. Avoiding a couple of thick, wall-like spider webs, he sat down on one of the dilapidating steps underneath the porch.

At about 5:30, a white Lexus came zooming down the street and parked along the curb in front of the house. The driver, an Asian man in his forties, got out and slammed the car door.

"Nate Hollis?" he asked, pushing up his wraparound sunglasses so they rested at his receding hairline. He had a top-of-the-line wireless Bluetooth wrapped around his ear.

Hollis nodded.

"Richard Yamamoto." He extended his hand and gave Hollis a firm but not too firm handshake. Under his other arm was a manila folder.

"Is Monica still coming?" Hollis asked.

"She called. Can't make it because something came up at work."

Figures, thought Hollis. He was disappointed, but this was a paying gig. He was wrong to expect anything more.

Richard went up the porch stairs and gathered up the mail on the welcome mat. Out of his pocket came a set of keys with a red tag and number, as if they were from a valet. Just how many keys did this man handle a day? Hollis wondered.

The door looked like it was recently rekeyed, and Richard was able to easily get the door unlocked. Hollis stepped into the house behind him, a stale smell immediately hitting his nostrils.

"Excuse the mess. I live in Orange County. Don't have the opportunity to come out to the old neighborhood anymore."

Mess was right. Stacks of old newspapers – both *L.A. Times* and Little Tokyo daily newspaper, *The Rafu Shimpo*, stood like sentries throughout the house. A layer of dust covered all the tchotchkes assembled on every flat surface. "As you can see, my mother was a bit of a pack rat. I told her to throw out this junk and I could set her up in one of my apartments in Newport. But no, she had to stay close to what she knew."

Richard was able to clear a path to the dining room and pushed aside an old box of chocolate-covered macadamia nuts off the table's surface.

"Monica said that you were good," Richard said. "And that you'll give me a competitive rate."

Okay, so it's going to be like that, Hollis thought. Always the rich folks were looking out for the best deal. Hollis put out a number and they haggled a bit before decided on five hundred dollars, half of it received today.

Opening up the manila folder that he had brought with him, Richard laid some bank statements on the table. "Here's the check deposit right here. Twenty thousand dollars. And look, once a week over the course of five months, one thousand dollars was withdrawn."

The withdrawals were like clockwork. The branch was the one on First Street in Little Tokyo. Parking was shit around there.

"My mother couldn't get to the bank on her own. That's about the time she had a stroke; she could barely walk. She got around in a wheelchair. It was Yolanda that took her."

"Have you talked with her?"

"I've tried, but she's changed her cell phone number. This is her last known address."

Hollis looked at the digits and street name scrawled on a square Post-it note. "I know that neighborhood." It was a couple of blocks south of the now shuttered Holiday Bowl on Crenshaw Boulevard.

"I went by the house."

"I'm sure that went well."

"I certainly wasn't welcomed. A young guy opened the door but claimed that Yolanda didn't live there any more and he didn't know where she was. I knew that he was covering for her."

Hollis jotted the address in his notebook. "Okay, I'll check it out."

"Maybe you can shake her down or something."

"Just how old is Yolanda?"

"She's probably in her seventies."

I don't rough up seventy-year-old women, Hollis thought. "I'll do what I can."

"Well, I expect that you'll do more than that." Richard opened up his checkbook. "I'm depending on you getting back my twenty grand."

***

Hollis thought about calling Monica and asking her how well she really knew Richard Yamamoto, the son of her second grandmother. But since he had already cashed Richard's check, he figured there was no point. If Yolanda really took Michi Yamamoto's reparations' money, then she probably didn't have much to show for it almost a decade later. But if she admitted it, maybe members of her family would be willing to throw in a few bucks to keep their matriarch from going to jail.

After going to his bank, he went to the last known address of Yolanda Washington. He parked across the street a few doors down and waited, his cell phone at his ear. Fortunately this was a neighborhood in which a black man sitting by himself in a car talking on the phone was an everyday occurrence.

A service truck left the driveway around eleven o'clock. The advertisement on the door featured the name of a plumbing company and a phone number. Hollis quickly jotted it down. About a half an hour later, a sedan parked in front of the house and an older black woman with glasses and white relaxed hair emerged from the passenger side. "I'll see you later," she said to the driver. "Thanks for the ride."

After the sedan left and the old woman was in the house, Hollis jogged across the street and approached the door. He rang the doorbell one time.

The door opened but the security gate remained in place.

"Yes."

"Are you Yolanda Washington?"

"Who are you?"

"Nate Hollis."

"Do I know you?" Yolanda reminded Hollis of one of his older aunties. This was a potential thief, he tried to tell himself, but it was hard to shake off the familiarity.

"No, ma'am. I'm a friend of a friend of Michi Yamamoto. The Japanese woman who lived in Boyle Heights."

"Anyone who is a friend of a friend of Michi, is a friend of mine. C'mon in."

They sat in the well-appointed living room. The hardwood floor looked polished of any nicks and scratches.

"I'm a private investigator. Michi Yamamoto had told people that she didn't want anything to do with reparations for the Japanese in government camps during World War II but now in her bank statements, it shows that she did. Only thing is, what happened to the money?"

Yolanda, who was in an easy chair across from Hollis, sighed. "This is the son's doing, right? He's the one who's opening this up after poor Michi is dead."

Leaning forward on the couch. Hollis transferred the weight from his back to his legs.

"He never visited her during the year or two I looked after her while she was recovering from her stroke. Do you know what he does?"

"He owns some real estate properties."

"Ha! He's a slumlord. I bet he didn't tell you that."

"He said that he had some units in Newport Beach."

"Newport, ha! In Costa Mesa, if even that. He buys up apartment buildings in these poor neighborhoods, never fixes them up, and then charges an arm and a leg. Then as the neighborhood improves, he sells the land to the highest bidder."

Hollis was surprised that Monica, being a Legal Aid attorney, wasn't up on her childhood neighbor's shenanigans. Of course, with shell companies, it was sometimes difficult to discover who owned what. "Mrs. Washington, I hear you, but again, that's beside the point. Did you know about the money? She was regularly taking out one thousand dollars a week over the course of five months. She was confined to a wheelchair at the time, so I think that she needed some help. I think that help was you."

"Look, her money was her business. Yes, I took her to the bank but I wasn't policing what she was spending money on. She could have had a private Chippendale's session in the middle of the night for all I knew."

Hollis stared into Yolanda's eyes, trying to determine if there was any deceit behind them. But he could only see the eyes of his Grand-aunt Ruth. Dammit, Hollis, he chided himself, what the hell kind of P.I. are you?

He wasn't able to get much more out of Yolanda. When he returned to the Dart, a couple of young kids were standing beside it, admiring the recent detailing he had done on the car. He was going to tell them not to touch his ride but what the hell, if you see something so pretty, how can you help yourself not to?

Before he left the Crenshaw area, he called Monica and left a message on her voicemail. "I think that you better check out your friend, Richard Yamamoto. He's done some shady things in the past, especially related to low-income apartments."

Hollis eventually got on the 110 and headed for Gardena. He needed to maximize his two hundred and fifty dollars, but more importantly he needed to drum up some more clients. The Hustler Casino, which had recently opened, was the spot for people in trouble who were looking to get out of it. The Compton public defenders hung out there, too, but it was a little too early in the day for them. He was at the blackjack table, losing about a fifth of his money, when his cell phone vibrated.

"I think I got you involved in something that I shouldn't have," Monica said, not even bothering to say hello.

You are telling me, he thought, walking into a quieter spot. "How about we meet for dinner tonight?" he suggested.

Surprisingly, she agreed. Since she had to appear in court in downtown Los Angeles, they settled on a local Mexican seafood favorite, La Serenata De Garibaldi, in Boyle Heights. Hollis, who wasn't a fish lover, thought it was just okay, but he wasn't going there for the food.

Monica was already seated, munching on some tortilla chips, when he arrived that evening.

"You're right," she said. "In the past, we've represented clients who had a beef with the Richard Yamamoto's real estate company, Mountain Source. He arbitrarily kicked people out of their apartments and broke leases. It was before my time with Legal Aid, so I never dealt with his tenants. His properties are all now pretty much in Orange County. I got more curious as to why he even called me, so I called his younger sister, Janice, in Cerritos."

The waiter then came by their table to take their order. Hollis stayed safe with the carnitas, which didn't win him any points with Monica. They both ordered margaritas on the rocks.

"They've been feuding ever since their mother passed away," Monica continued. "Richard is the executor of the estate and has already used up all his mother's liquid assets. Now he wants to sell his share of the house, but Janice doesn't have enough money to buy him out. I think they will be headed to a forced sale."

So apparently Richard Yamamoto had a lot, but he owed a whole lot more. That twenty thousand dollars probably looked like free money that could buy him some time from his creditors.

"Do you know where Richard lives?"

Monica shook her head. "Somewhere in the OC. But not sure exactly where. I can ask his sister and get back to you, but she was pretty upset about the whole thing. I don't know if she'll accept another call from me."

The night ended a little too early for Hollis. Monica said that she had an 8 AM meeting the next day. They walked out together to the small parking lot in the back.

After paying the parking valet for both their cars, Hollis walked Monica to hers. He wanted to make a move but he didn't want to rush it. Turned out he didn't have to be in his head so much. While standing in a dark corner of lot by the gate, Monica's soft lips were on his.

"Salty," she said, smiling, after their long kiss.

They sure were.

***

That night Hollis tried to figure out what he was going to do. He could drop the case, but that meant returning Richard his two hundred and fifty dollars and forgoing another two hundred and fifty. That would hurt financially, but he had been in worse situations before. But he didn't want to quite let go of this investigation. What was Michi Yamamoto doing with that cold, hard cash? It could have been for drug transactions, but the woman hardly fit the usual profile. If she was confined to a wheelchair, her caregiver had to know more than she shared.

The next morning, Hollis returned to Yolanda Washington's street and parked. The same plumbing truck was in the driveway and as it pulled out to leave, Hollis was able to see the driver, a young black man maybe in his late twenties. As the car headed toward the stop sign, Hollis got out and walked across the street. Before he made it to the other side, the truck had made a U-turn and sped right for him.

Hollis cursed and took a nose dive onto the sidewalk. Luckily he landed on a patch of dying grass instead of asphalt.

Leaving his truck in the middle of the street, the driver got out and stormed towards Hollis, who got to his feet. His opponent was small but muscular, probably developed from hours of manual labor.

"I heard about you and your classic car. What business do you have with my grandmother?"

Before Hollis could defend himself, either physically or verbally, Yolanda was out on the sidewalk beside them.

"It's all right, Eric, I got it covered," she said.

"No, it's not all right. I want to know what's going on."

"At least get your truck out of the middle of the street and come into the house where we can talk like civilized people."

They were back in the living room, only this time Yolanda was on the couch with Hollis while the grandson, wearing a uniform, glared at him from the easy chair.

Hollis introduced himself as a private investigator hired to look into what happened to the reparations that Michi Yamamoto had received ten years ago.

"I had a feeling that this story was going come out sometime," Yolanda said. She explained to her grandson that she had worked as a caregiver for a Japanese woman for a couple of years in Boyle Heights, where she had lived with her husband until the mid-1990s. "We were practically the only black people around at that time," she said. "But your grandfather had grown up there and we had a house, so it was definitely home."

She spoke slowly and deliberately, as if taking time would help her remember what happened ten years ago. "That Michi Yamamoto was a sweetheart. I don't know if you remember her, Eric."

"She'd always be coming by your house, bringing over food and vegetables."

"Ah, ha, that was her. I think after she recovered from her stroke, she felt beholden to me. That's how the Japanese are, very thankful people."

"What else did you do for her, Mrs. Washington?" Hollis asked.

"When I was watching her, it must have been in 1991 or so, maybe right before the riots, there was a story in the Japanese newspaper. I would always read to her the paper that she got in the mail. It was about an apartment building owner that was being investigated by the city for being a slumlord. Turned out that owner was her son, Richard Yamamoto. He sold it a few months later."

"She was so upset. I know that she wanted to tell him off, but she wasn't that good at talking at that time. I was afraid that she was going to have another stroke, right on the spot." Yolanda took a deep breath and folded her hands together. "Michi made me find out who each of those tenants were. I had to go by that apartment building and it was crazy as hell down there."

"I had twenty names, mostly all Latino. I had to find out where they moved to and that wasn't easy. Once a week, we'd go over to Japantown and take out another one thousand dollars and I'd deliver the money like Santa Claus, only sometimes they'd be wondering who I was and what I had to do with the apartment."

"I can't believe she'd be asking you to do something like that." Eric shook his head.

"No, you don't understand. Michi was a true friend. Sometimes things weren't going that great with your grandfather – this is way before her stroke when your father was just a boy – and she'd sit there and listen. She never told me what to do. But she understood what I was going through. Just her listening helped me get through the rough patches. I would have done anything for her."

Hearing such frank talk about his grandmother's personal life made Eric feel uncomfortable. He took out his phone and glanced at the display. "I better get going to work, Grandma. Are you sure that you're going to be okay with this guy?"

"I'm perfectly fine," she said.

Eric rose, giving Hollis one last stare, a warning not to mess with his kin.

After her grandson left, Yolanda's shoulders slumped. "What are you going to do? If the son finds out that I was part of this, he'll probably sue my butt."

Hollis wasn't quite sure how he was going to handle the situation.

"He was supposed to pay me, you know, for taking care of Michi. But he didn't. The cheapskate. The daughter who lives in Cerritos was the one who eventually offered me some money. I told her that it was okay; that Michi was a friend, so I didn't mind. Good thing she recovered. That lady was a fighter."

"You know where any of those people who you gave money to live today?"

Yolanda pursed her lips. "Actually, just one. We became kind of friends. He was a young kid back then. Maybe only seventeen. He was being raised by his grandmother, who was having health problems of her own. I felt sorry for him so I tried to keep my eye out for him. It didn't work out so well because he got into some trouble. Robbed a convenience store and ended up shooting a customer's foot in the process. He didn't know what he was doing. I sent him a couple of letters and he let me know that he was getting out a couple of months ago. He's in some kind of transitional housing in South Central. I have his phone number."

***

It wasn't that difficult to track Richard Yamamoto's home address. Hollis had a contact at the Los Angeles County Assessor's office who called in a favor with the someone in Orange County. He set up his Garmin GPS in his car and followed the computer voice down three freeways until he was finally in Newport Beach, a couple of blocks from the water.

The house was painted white and blue and looked like it belonged along the coast of New England rather than in California. A flag with illustrated pumpkins waved in the sea breeze.

Before Hollis even reached the porch, the door flung open. "Hey, what are you doing here?" said Richard. "I thought that we would be meeting at my mother's house later today."

"I was in the neighborhood, so I figured that I would give you an update on the case."

"Honey, who is it?" A female voice said from one of the back rooms.

"Nobody," Richard said, closing the door behind him and ushering Hollis towards the garage.

This is the way you are going to play it, thought Hollis. "This whole thing about your mother's reparations money. I investigated it and she spent it the way she wanted." He went on to explain how she had paid relocation money to the twenty families affected by Mountain Source's eviction back in 1992.

Richard was not happy with Hollis's discovery. "I paid you to investigate Yolanda Washington and get my money."

"You paid me to find out what happened to the reparations

money. And it wasn't yours to keep. It was your mother's to use as she thought fit and unfortunately, she chose to spend it to clear your sorry ass. The rest of my fee, please. Two hundred and fifty dollars."

"You're not going to get any more money out of me."

"That's too bad. Maybe the others will feel differently."

Richard stopped dead in his tracks. He was listening.

"There are others who will want to send their regards to you. In person. One of them just got out of San Quentin." It didn't hurt to embellish some. "Another spent some time in Corcoran. And Yolanda's grandson seemed mighty interested in talking with you too. I'll just pass along your home address to all of them."

"You wouldn't."

"I bet your neighbors will be wondering why all you are getting all these uninvited visitors. I'm sure the rest of your household might be, too."

Richard's face was beet red. He got out his money clip, counted two-hundred-and-sixty dollars and pushed it in Hollis's right palm.

"I think I have change," Hollis pulled out his wallet.

Richard was ready to explode. "Just get the hell out of my house. And I never want to see you again."

***

Later, Hollis celebrated the successful culmination of the case in Monica's bedroom.

"I don't think Richard Yamamoto will want to talk to you anymore," he said as they both lay underneath the sheets facing the ceiling.

"That's fine with me. He already gave me an earful," she said.

"Really?" Hollis turned to Monica.

"I told him that he had nothing to complain about it. That it was all about reparations, anyhow."

WHITE OUT

by
Sara Paretsky

I

"You need a little something to breathe life back into those frozen lungs of yours. Scotch? Rye?"

Nate Hollis hadn't noticed the woman until she swept over to him, the gold sequins in her jacket glinting and winking under the lamps. Nate's eyes were already raw from the wind; the psychedelic show made him wince. Her cornrow braids accentuated her Nefertiti profile. This was Amara Herrare, owner of Club 823.

Clutch Hollis had tried to talk his grandson out of the trip – "It's January! You any idea what that feels like? You going in that skinny windbreaker? Get yourself some polar fleece if you're planning on coming home with the jewels intact!" – but when he learned where Nate was starting his investigation, Clutch pushed the National Association of Black Bar Owners handbook into his duffel bag.

"I want a detailed report on 823. Every detail, down to whether she uses tap or filtered to water her whisky. That place is a legend: Eddie Vinson, Charlie Parker, Phineas Newborn, they all played there."

No trip to Chicago is complete without a visit to Amara Herrare's Club 823 (823 S Wabash). Legend has it that Herrare's mother won the club in a poker game with that old wily coyote Con Stutzman, but whatever the truth, this is the place for real jazz and blues in Chicago, not the watered down stuff they play for the white tourists on Hubbard Street.

Nate had read this on the flight out. In the bar, looking at Herrare's regal face and her long lithe body, he wondered if Clutch had slept with her at some bar owner's meeting.

"Local brew." Nate's voice came out as a harsh mumble, inaudible over the music. There wasn't a live act tonight, but

Herrare had an old jukebox against the far wall which kept spinning the icons who used to play the club.

Nate had looked at the forecast online but he hadn't been able to imagine what nine degrees felt like. Now he knew. Like being flayed all over his body. He hated to admit Clutch had been right. When his grandfather tried to buy him a down parka, he'd said, "I'm not planning on being outside, Clutch. Airplane to rental car, rental car to heated buildings."

What Nate hadn't visualized was the seven-minute wait outside for the rental car bus, or the two-block walk to Club 823. Two blocks, quarter of a mile, ninety seconds. If it had been another quarter, he'd be dead, for sure.

He cleared his throat and repeated his request for beer.

Herrare studied his face. "You need a boilermaker to warm you. Drink this first."

She splashed Russell's Reserve into a glass and put it in front of Nate before twisting the cap from a bottle of Hophazardly. Before Nate could object, she'd moved off to pour a Jack Daniels for a white man at the end of the bar who seemed to have melted into his stool. She gave his shoulder a commiserating pat, then slipped out through the open end of the bar to work the room. She knew who wanted to be left alone, who wanted a little light chat. All the time she kept an eye on the room, nodding at her bartender when someone's glass was empty or they were moving restlessly in their seats, wanting the check.

Lakers and Bulls were on a screen over the bar. Not a pretty sight tonight.

When Herrare moved back behind the bar, running a cloth over a wet spot left by a glass of water, Nate caught her eye.

She pointed at the empty Hophazardly bottle, eyebrows raised in question. When he nodded, she conjured a second bottle.

"What brings you to Chicago, Angel?"

"Angel?" he echoed.

"It's not enough that you have an LAX claim check on your bag, but every time we block one of Randle's shots, you wince."

"You should be in law enforcement," Nate said. "Either that or teaching eighth-grade social studies."

"And I reckon you're in law enforcement – only reason a man with your traps checks a duffel bag is because he's got a licensed

165

weapon in it. You've come to clean up Chicago? You need more than a gun and muscle here, Angel. Maybe a duffel bag full of federal warrants."

Nate rolled the bottle between his palms. His hands had warmed enough that he could feel cold again and he didn't like it.

"I made a mistake about the beer. Let me have a Macallan." When Amara had poured, he said, "I'm looking for Claudette Ng."

The Macallan bottle came to a full stop on its way back to the shelf. The gold sequins winked and twinkled under the lights, and then Amara had put the bottle away, turned back to Nate and said lightly, "If you think she's here, you're welcome to look around."

She started toward the Jack Daniels end of the bar but Nate leaned across the zinc counter. "Ms. Herrare, I flew 2,000 miles and froze my ass to talk to you. If I've put a foot wrong, I didn't do it on purpose: Ng lists you as next of kin."

The Nefertiti profile was colder than the outside air. "We haven't been in touch for years. If you flew to Chicago thinking you'd find her at 823, you wasted the fare and the time. Go check into that Hilton at the airport – you won't have to go outside, just walk out of bed onto the first LA-bound flight you can find."

Amara was still smiling; only Ludwig, her bartender, noticed the tendons standing out along the jaw line.

"Can I tell you the whole story, before you impale me?"

"As long as the punchline doesn't include me giving a rat's toenail about where Claudette Ng is parking herself these days."

"Ng's been shooting a film for Vanguard these days."

"Not interested." Amara started to turn away.

"I have a friend there." Nate spoke to his glass of whisky, but raised his voice: Amara was listening, just pretending not to. "LaWanda Rhames. Ng saw me one day last week when I was checking in with Rhames about something else. She went to Rhames after I left and said she knew something curious about an open investigation of mine."

"You LAPD?" Amara asked, her back still turned to him.

"Private," Nate said. "But PI's have open cases, just like cops. We just don't get paid for sifting through them. Ng called me on Friday; I called back, left a couple of messages, finally had a message from her that she'd meet me Tuesday at the set before she was due to shoot. I was there, she wasn't, she never showed,

LaWanda gave me her home address. She'd cleared out. A guy I know ran her credit cards – she'd booked a flight to Chicago early Tuesday morning. So here I am, wanting to talk to her."

Amara left him to deal with a couple of new arrivals, apparently cherished clients, since Ludwig was mixing a martini and a margarita while Amara took the couple's coats. Once they had their drinks, she toured the room before coming back to Nate.

"Your open case must be pretty intense to bring you out here without stopping for a coat, let alone a pair of mittens," Amara said.

"Vanguard wants her back," Nate admitted. "They're shooting some warrior-chick flick and Ng is the Burmese princess holding the English off at the Irrawaddy. They've shot half her scenes, so if they have to scrub her, they need to start again from ground zero. They can't afford it."

"Board of Trade is only five blocks away: I hear tales of corporate financial agony every day of the week. You have to develop a shell, Angel, or you'd be breaking your heart over money losses 24/7." She fluttered her improbably long eyelashes in mock grief.

"Her agent said she lists you as next of kin."

"That made sense when she lived in Chicago, but we've been out of touch since she moved to Hollywood. She probably forgot she'd put me on her forms. There was a Carson Dobb she was hanging with when we last spoke. I'd ask him."

"Dobb. Shit!" Why the fuck hadn't LaWanda told him about Dobb?

"Shit, what?" Amara demanded.

"You never heard of Dobb? You are one lucky woman. Word on the street says even the Russian mob is scared of him. If your cousin –"

"Not my cousin." Amara's smile twisted into a sneer. "Claudette's a little more than kin. Definitely less than kind."

"More than – oh." Of course Clutch had never slept with Amara. Was there any way Nate could have been less prepared when he got on that plane this morning? No winter coat or gloves: check. No knowledge of Carson Dobb's relations with Ng: check. Not realizing Herrare was a dike and Ng had been her lover: check. Not knowing what LaWanda Rhames really had on her mind when she sent him out to this deep freeze. Check and double-check.

He was fucked if it was going to be check-mate, though.

"If she didn't come to you, who else does Ng know in Chicago she'd turn to?"

Amara shrugged; she'd lost touch with Ng, she didn't know who Ng knew any more.

The bar was starting to fill as the theatres emptied. Amara turned away from Nate and began making air kisses with her regulars.

II

The Macallan, the Russell's Reserve, two beers, not so smart coming at the tag-end of a day that had begun fourteen hours ago. Nate had to keep getting out of the car and running in place to stay awake. Cops swung by, shone their spots on him. Fuck. That's what he needed, trigger-happy cop putting sixteen rounds in him for running in place on a January night. He got back in the car and made a wide loop around the bar, four blocks south, over to the lake, back up to Congress, over to the small street on the west side of the bar where a cab rank had enough action to give him some cover.

At two in the morning, the lights began to go out in 823. The last of the determined drinkers tottered out, and five minutes later, Amara and Ludwig emerged. A sedan pulled up. Ludwig put Amara into it with the tenderness of a Geary's sales clerk handling Baccarat glassware. Ludwig climbed into the front seat; the sedan drove to an L station five blocks away and decanted him there before swinging east and then south onto Lake Shore Drive.

They had the lake on their left all the way south. It wasn't water but a sea of ink covered by a layer of crushed ice. It felt ominous in a way the ocean never did. The Pacific was powerful, it could crush you—but it was exhilarating. Michigan was like some cold night crawler that would slither out and strangle you. Amara's apartment was directly across the road from the water.

Nate watched the limo driver escort Amara into the building. He waited in the lobby until the elevator arrived before driving off.

Two or three insomniacs had their lights on but the building was essentially dark; when a light came on at the top of the building, seventeenth floor, second window from the left, Nate knew Herrare had reached home. Shadow play: Amara's image, elongated into something out of Edward Gorey, arms with a condor's wingspan waving in anger; a shorter figure, visible only from the waist up, hand on hip: belligerent. He didn't know if Herrare lived alone, but this wasn't a feel-good encounter she was having.

It was four in the morning; he'd been up for twenty hours and was in that numb place where he felt as though he was completely alone on the planet. He'd passed a motel along the road; he backtracked until he found the neon light blinking half-heartedly. The perfect place for him to stop, a motel that couldn't tell if it was alive or dead. He roused the night clerk, not easily, and asked for room as far away from the water as possible.

III

"I hate everything about this damned town," Nate shouted at LaWanda. "It's colder than Dick Cheney's heart, they cheered in the bar when the Lakers lost, they have a lake that will eat you alive. But most of all, I hate you not telling me that Carson Dobb was bankrolling Ng."

"Not bankrolling her, Hollis," LaWanda said. "Yes, he bought her that house up in Crystal Canyon, but we're paying her a pretty handsome fee. Which we're losing every day we don't –"

"Jesus H. Christ, I do not care about your shooting schedule. If she's hiding from Dobb, then all I'm going to do by finding her is put a bullseye over her eyes, and probably mine as well. And I'm sure you have insurance for your principals disappearing, dying, committing murder or getting axed by the Mob, so don't bleat at me."

"Monday morning you came as desperate to find Ng as Derek Carr looking for a wide-out. I paid your freight to Chicago as a favor, Hollis. Stop whining, it isn't attractive."

"Tell me this, Sunshine: what hold does Dobb have over Ng?"

"Ever occur to you it might be vice-versa? Might be why girlfriend blew Dodge."

LaWanda cut the connection. Nate had slept until ten, woke to find snow falling outside. Falling, that was a ludicrous word. Woke up to find snow raging from the heavens, rising from the ground, scudding in from the ice-clumped lake, cutting his eyelids when he went out to see if his car would start. The motel's building engineer took pity on him and drove him in a truck to a store where he got a down parka, boots, gloves – and a shovel so he could dig himself out when he got stuck in a snowdrift. Nate bitterly noted the "when," not "if."

Around one, when it became clear that Mother Nature hated

him and the storm was going to last at least until the next morning, he dug himself out of the parking lot and slipped and slid back down to Sixty-Eighth Street, where Amara Herrare lived. He found a clear place in the road that wouldn't block traffic – no one was going to get close to the curb today – and called Club 823. Amara was there, brought in no doubt by bulldozer. He hung up without speaking to her.

Her building had a doorman, skinny man, maybe eighty, whose skin had mottled grey with age, but he held himself erect. When Nate asked if he'd let Claudette Ng in yesterday, the doorman said, "Who Ms. Herrare lets into her home is none of your concern, young man. You best be on your way before you find yourself in trouble."

Nate looked behind him at the white air outside. Even if cops came readily to this Black neighborhood on clear days – always a big "if," no matter what city you were in – no one was going anywhere fast today. He laughed: he had to respect the guy, who must have realized Nate could carry him under one arm if he wanted to.

He tried to cajole the doorman with the truth, at least as far as he knew or believed it – that Ng had fled LA ahead of a Mob heavy, that her presence in Amara's apartment could put Club 823's owner at risk, that he, Nate, needed to talk to Ng about valuable information she had.

"It's a good story, son," the doorman said. "Day like today, without much action, I like a good story. But whether Ms. Ng is here or not, whether Ms. Herrare knows or not, none of that is your business until Ms. Herrare lets it be your business. You go on back to Los Angeles. It will all look clearer in the sunshine."

A big man came into the building, carrying a hundred pound bag of rock salt over his shoulder. His parka was unzipped and his bronze face was wet, not with snow as Nate first thought, but sweat.

"Got the parking lot dug out, Zeke. Coming down an inch an hour, they said on the radio, have to go out again in an hour. Better check the radiator in Ms. Beal's place, leaking, her daughter told me this morning." He jerked his head toward Nate, eyebrows raised.

"He's a private investigator, in from Los Angeles. Best look out, Rainier, he might start investigating you just to keep his hand in."

The banter had an edge; Rainier would take Nate on if he tried to bull past Zeke into the building. After a few minutes Nate went back out into the storm. He sat in the car with the heater and the wipers on, studied the building. He was across the street and could barely make out what units were showing light. Seventeenth floor, second window from the left, showed a faint glow, he thought.

The building had a service entrance, no doubt where Rainier broke private investigators into his soup, like crackers, but he was going up to Ms. Beal's place to check her radiator. Make hay while the storm blows.

He slipped and slid his way to the back of the building. Oranges, tank tops, in-line skaters, all that was happening at home at the same time he was freezing and snow blind in Chicago. How could those universes exist simultaneously?

Rainier had left the service door unlocked, one tiny mercy in a world of misery. Night seemed to be coming on: not that you could tell day from night in a blizzard, but some additional menace seemed to lurk behind the swirling white.

Inside the open door were at least a dozen hundred-pound sacks of rock salt. Nate tensed at the sound of voices, then realized it was Rainier's television.

He slipped past Rainier's open cubbyhole, found the service elevator, rode it up to seventeen. It was quiet in the hallway; the old building had thick walls and the shrieking of the wind didn't penetrate. The silence felt luxurious. Warm entryway, thick carpet, he could have curled up on the floor and slept.

There were two apartments on the floor, an entry door on either side of the elevator. Herrare's was the one that faced north. He knocked on the door. No answer. He tried the door. Locked.

"Claudette – it's Nate Hollis. LaWanda sent me out here to talk to you, see when you're coming back to the set."

Another long minute passed, and then a lock turned and Ng had the door open the width of a chain bolt. She was holding a gun, its barrel too close to the opening in the doorway.

"Put the damned gun down, Claudette," Nate said. "I'm not going to kill you, much as I feel like it."

"You go back to LA, Hollis, and try minding your own

business."

"Me?" Nate was furious. "You're the one who involved me, remember? You called me. You said you had news for me about my father's murder. Remember that?"

"But –"

"Put the damned gun down."

Claudette looked at the hand holding the Luger as if it were a strange appendage that had just appeared on her arm. She lowered the weapon and undid the chain bolt. Nate slipped inside and locked the door again.

"Now. What happened between Sunday night, when you gave me an Oscar-winning performance of a woman who knew more than she should reveal, and tonight when you're looking more like a starlet in a B gangster flick?"

"I got homesick for Chicago," Claudette said.

Nate gestured toward the snow, which was beating on the window as if it were a live beast trying to break in. "Right. This kind of weather tugs at the heartstrings when you're sunbathing by Carson Dobb's swimming pool."

"And I missed Amara."

"Don't shit an old hand, Ng. You're not high on Amara Herrare's hit parade and you didn't miss Chicago. Dobb threaten you?"

He paused, thinking it over. "Dobb is the person with the information, isn't he? And he heard you talking to me and told you what he did to naughty starlets who leak bedroom secrets. And you thought the best thing you could do was to put Amara Herrare's life in danger. You'd already screwed her once, why not do it up royally, put her in Carson Dobb's gunsights?"

Claudette flinched. "You make it sound so harsh, Nate, but you're not really a harsh person, not deep down."

Nate groaned. "What's cheesier than a B flick? I've watched Mary Astor deliver that line to Bogie, oh, maybe seventy-three times, and believe me, sister, she puts it over way more convincingly."

Claudette bit her lip and turned away.

"Right. Now we get the, 'if you really loved me' sequence. Is that what you laid on Amara Herrare last night? She must have been pleased as Santa Monica in a tsunami when she got home from work and found you on her divan here." Nate gestured at the pale green sofa behind Claudette. There was a nest of blankets and shawls; she must have been dozing when Nate was pounding on the door.

"Now tell me what you learned about Earl. And no trembling with the lower lip because *believe* me, I've seen every change rung on that note you can imagine and probably a few you can't."

"No matter what I say, you're going to make fun of me," Claudette said.

"Not if you give me a few straight sentences without lies or histrionics."

Claudette studied his face and apparently decided he couldn't be cajoled; she went back to the green sofa and sat on the edge of the middle cushion, the gun in her hands but pointed at the floor.

"I don't see Carson that often – I wasn't born yesterday, I know he has three or four gift houses up in the canyons." Her lip curled. "Like a Mormon without all the legal hassles, his wives. He likes – never mind what he likes. It was a good deal for me when I was cut from *Fly By Night* and couldn't find another gig. I won't say I went in with my eyes wide open because two years ago, I was ignorant about a lot of things you can see in Hollywood when you know where to look – but I knew enough, I'll say that."

Nate pulled an armchair in from the edge of the rug so that he was almost touching Ng's knees. Switched on a second lamp so he could study her face, a perfect oval, the color of an iced latte, thick black hair pulled away in a knot, the hazel eyes slightly hooded, a micron slanted – the ideal face for today's Hollywood – race-neutral, traditional Eurasian beauty.

"When you came on the Irrawaddy set last Friday, I told Carson about it – he's nervous about law enforcement."

"Smart man," Nate growled. "What'd you tell him?"

"The truth – I had no idea why you were there, you'd been in meeting with LaWanda. He was letting me borrow this for the show –"

Claudette pulled a necklace from inside her sweater. It was a ruby, about the size and color of a ripe tomato.

"What the – why the fuck are you lugging that around?"

"It's valuable," Claudette said. "It's the Irrawaddy Ruby – when Carson learned what the movie was, who I'd been cast to play, he got it out of the vault – he said it was too amazing a coincidence to pass up. When I told him I'd seen you at Vanguard, he asked why; I told him I thought maybe LaWanda was hiring extra security."

Nate groaned. "Are you as stupid as you act, or do you act stupid because you're so beautiful and acting stupid keeps people from being too jealous?"

A mischievous smile played briefly on Ng's face. "I'm lucky to be born like this, and unlucky, too – you never know whether you're any good at what you do, or if you're getting by on your looks. As far as the Irrawaddy Ruby goes, I guess I was stupid. I thought if I was going to be on the run from Carson, I needed something to pay my bills. Trying to pawn this is like trying to pawn the Empire State Building. And, of course, nothing was more likely to bring Carson looking for me."

A variety of highly-colored responses went through Nate's mind, but he only said drily, "Yes, indeed. But what made you call me, and then what made you run for cover?"

"One of the guys who works for him, one of his smart muscles, Carson calls him – Sean O'Reilly – he showed up. I was going out to the pool when I heard them talking there. I don't like O'Reilly, he always looks at me like he can see me tied to a table while he chooses which blade to slit me with, so I was turning to go back when I realized they were talking about me, about you, really. 'Bitch knows Hollis?' O'Reilly asked, and gave an ugly laugh. 'She know about you and Earl?'"

Nate was impressed: he knew O'Reilly, no one who tap-danced around the edge of law and order in LA could avoid him, and with a simple change of posture, change of accent, Claudette Ng brought him into the room. So not just sex and beauty, girl could act.

"That was when I called you. Everyone in L.A. knows you're trying to find out what happened to Earl. What I didn't know was that Carson installed tracking software on my phone." Ng shuddered. "After you and I set up the meet for Tuesday, Carson came for me, wanted to know what kind of eavesdropping bitch I was. He had O'Reilly with him. I threw up on his shoes and while he was screaming and yelling – custom brogues from Vienna, thirty thousand a pair – I ran."

"You threw up on his shoes?" Nate blinked. He wondered if the storm and sleep loss were affecting his brain.

"It's not exactly a party trick – I went to Northwestern on a swim scholarship. They weighed us before each meet and if we were over what the coach expected, they had us barf it up. My parents were boat people, my mother was French, but she stayed on after she married my father. She was obsessed with wanting never to be caught again behind enemy lines. I never go anywhere without mapping an escape route. She drilled it into me from the time I was two. I incorporated willful barfing into my escape plans, that's all."

She laughed humorlessly at Nate's shocked expression. "All athletes in sports where weight matters learn how. We had competitions with the gymnasts and the cheerleaders."

Nate thought nothing could faze him, but the image of rows of female athletes over the toilets – no, he'd never be able to watch the Olympics again if he dwelled on that.

Over the howling of the storm, Nate heard a more ominous sound: someone working on the apartment door. No time to wonder about Zeke and Rainier. He was pulling out his gun when Ng tugged his arm.

"Escape route. There's always an escape route."

She darted through the sitting room's far door. Nate hesitated a moment, heard the door splinter. Last stands were for Custer and other reckless white boys.

He found Ng in the kitchen, pulling on sheepskin boots, already swathed in scarves and mittens. She had the door open and was lowering herself to the fire escape while Nate was still tugging on his gloves and wondering if she was crazy or he was. A shot whined past his ear. He followed her out the kitchen door and slammed it shut.

It was night and white and deadly. Ice on the iron bars, impossible to make out Claudette Ng below him. As soon as he grabbed the first rung of the ladder, the wind slammed him against the fire escape and then tried to blow him away from it. He climbed down, one dogged leg at a time, wondering if he'd find Ng dead on the sidewalk when he reached the bottom.

His ears were throbbing, his eyes were blearing, his lungs could barely manage the effort of taking frozen air, warming it enough for his heart and letting it go again. He thought spring would come and they would find his body frozen to the ladder. He was barely able to follow the angles of the ladder, but suddenly found himself on a platform, Ng's small ice-covered body waiting for him.

She grabbed his right arm and tried to pull him into the apartment next to the platform. It was dark, but it was warm. Nate wanted to sit on the floor and sob. No wind, no snow, warmth.

"Escape route. Eleventh floor, empty apartment." Ng said. "I unlocked the back door after Amara left for work. Now we watch to see if our friends keep going to the bottom. If they do, then – do we follow them down, or hole up here?"

"We might even alert Amara to the fact that someone busted in her front door," Nate said sardonically.

"Right. You get to do that." Claudette snapped.

"No, Sunshine. You do that."

Two large bodies had landed on the platform. One of them fumbled with the door and Nate opened it fast, shoved it into them, knocking them off balance. One man fell, the other grabbed a railing and kept his balance. Hands scrabbled at Nate's ankles. He kicked backwards, connected with bone, then grappled with the man at the railing. They struggled on the icy platform, neither able to land a punch in the dark, when the man slipped, and fell backwards into the white air, giving a scream that Nate thought would stay with him forever.

The man he'd kicked was coming back to life, throwing punches at Nate's knees. Nate grabbed his hands and wrenched the gloves from them, tossing them into the whiteness. He backed into the empty kitchen. The punk on the platform was howling. "You mother-fucking stamen snarfing son of a, let me in, you took my gloves, I can't climb."

"Like that's my problem," Nate snarled to himself.

He stumbled to the sink, turned on the tap, drank deeply.

"I'm going down, see what happened to Zeke and Rainier," he told Claudette. "You call the cops on our diver and tell them we need a welcome committee for the dude who's freezing his nuts off out there."

IV

"What about the ruby?" Amara asked. She was perched on a stool next to him, the gold feathers in her cornrows adding eight inches to her height.

"Fake," Nate grinned, savoring the Macallan. The eighteen-year, better than the older casks, smooth as gold. "LaWanda knows that your friend Claudette has limited impulse control, as the modern LA jargon puts it. First thing she did when Claudette started flaunting it on the set was get a copy made. She hired me to switch them out."

"So you really did come here to find her for Vanguard, not to recover the ruby?"

"Something like that. I put her on the plane this morning. What she does when she gets to LA is between her and LaWanda."

"And Zeke and Rainier are recovering nicely," Amara said. "Thank goodness Dobb was so anxious to get up to my place he didn't stop to see if he'd killed Rainier."

The building super had taken a bullet in the shoulder. His heavy coat and his layers of muscle had kept the wound from being serious. Dobb's sidekick, Sean O'Reilly, had knocked Zeke out. The old man was badly shaken, but back on duty. Amara had covered his hospital bills, but Nate only learned that later.

"So – satisfactory all around," Amara asked. For once her eyes were on Nate, not roaming the room looking for trouble spots.

"Oh, yeah, except for damned near dying on your fire escape. And my car getting towed. If I never see a snowflake again, I will not miss it. Climate change can't heat up Chicago a second too fast for me."

"In that case, what's getting you down?" Amara asked.

Nate gave a rueful smile. "I wanted to know what Dobb knew about my old man. Who shot Earl, and why. And now I'll never know if he did. Bastard broke his neck falling off your fire escape. O'Reilly will live to be scum another day, but he doesn't know what Dobb knew, or at least he claims he doesn't."

Amara laughed, a huge bell that filled the bar and made people at the window tables smile without knowing what the joke was. "He did it to spite you, Angel, he did it to spite you."

ABOUT THE AUTHOR

Scott Adlerberg is the author of Jack Waters, a historical revenge thriller, from Broken River Books. His other books include the noir/fantasy novella Jungle Horses and the psychological thriller Graveyard Love. His short stories have appeared in Mystery Tribune, Thug Lit, All Due Respect, and the Protectors 2: Heroes: Stories to Benefit PROTECT anthology, and he is a regular contributor to sites such as Lithub and Criminal Element. Each summer, he hosts the Word for Word Reel Talks film commentary series in Manhattan. He lives in New York City.

Sarah M. Chen juggles several jobs including indie bookseller, transcriber, and insurance adjuster. She has published crime fiction short stories with Shotgun Honey, Crime Factory, Out of the Gutter, and Near to the Knuckle, among others. Cleaning Up Finn, her noir novella with All Due Respect Books, is an Anthony finalist and IPPY award winner. She's also co-editor of The Night of the Flood with E.A. Aymar, a "novel-in-stories" featuring fourteen thriller writers with an intro by Hank Phillippi Ryan. https://saramhchen.com

Sara Paretsky and her acclaimed PI, V.I. Warshawski, helped transform the role of women in contemporary crime fiction, beginning with the publication of her first novel, Indemnity Only, in 1982. Sisters in Crime, the advocacy organization she founded in 1986, has helped a new generation of crime writers to thrive. Among other awards, Paretsky holds the Cartier Diamond Dagger, MWA's Grand Master, and Ms. Magazine's Woman of the Year. Her PhD dissertation on 19th-Century US Intellectual History was recently published by the University of Chicago Press. Her most recent novel is Fallout, Harper-Collins 2017. Visit her at saraparetsky.com

Born under a bad sign, **Gary Phillips** must keep writing to forestall his appointment at the crossroads. He has written various novels, novellas, radio plays, scripts, graphic novels such as Vigilante: Southland, and published more than 60 short stories. Phillips has edited or co-edited several anthologies including the bestselling Orange County Noir, Black Pulp I & II, the critically praised The Obama Inheritance: Fifteen Stories of Conspiracy Noir, and Culprits, a linked anthology of a heist gone wrong.

Naomi Hirahara is the award-winning author of two mystery series. The third in her Mas Arai mysteries, SNAKESKIN SHAMISEN, won an Edgar Allan Poe for Best Paperback Original, while the first in her Officer Ellie Rush bicycle cop series, MURDER ON BAMBOO LANE, received a T. Jefferson Parker mystery award from the Southern California Independent Booksellers Association. Her novels have been translated in Japanese, Korean and for publication in 2016, French.
A former editor of The Rafu Shimpo newspaper in Los Angeles, she also has written several nonfiction books and noir short stories. Her book for young readers, 1001 CRANES, received Honorable Mention in Youth Literature from the Asian/Pacific American Librarians Association. Her second Officer Ellie Rush mystery, GRAVE ON GRAND AVENUE, was published in April 2015, while another short story, "Jigoku," was featured in the fantastical collection of crime stories related to Japan, HANZAI JAPAN (VIZ Media's Haikasoru) published in October 2015.

Phillip Drayer Duncan is the author of 4 published novels and 12 short stories. He has work published with Yard Dog Press, Pro Se Productions, and Seventh Star Press.
His earliest books were acted out with action figures and scribbled into notebooks. Today he uses a computer like a real grown up. He would probably still play with the action figures if people wouldn't think he was crazy. He may be the only author that's ever sponsored a race car. His greatest dream in life is to become a Jedi, but since that hasn't happened yet he focuses on writing.
For more information about Phillip Drayer Duncan...
PhillipDrayerDuncan.com

67132236R00111

Made in the USA
Middletown, DE
09 September 2019